A W

'Next time it's going to be me,' Shard Cortland told Elise uncompromisingly after her first husband Peter died—and perhaps she ought to have married Shard in the first place. So she married Shard at last. In the circumstances, they should both have been blissfully happy—so just what was going wrong with their marriage?

A WILDER SHORE

BY

DAPHNE CLAIR

MILLS & BOON LIMITED

15–16 BROOK'S MEWS
LONDON W1Y 1LF

First published 1980
Australian copyright 1980
Philippine copyright 1980
This edition 1980

© Daphne Clair 1980

ISBN 0 263 73333 5

Set in Linotype Pilgrim 10 on 11½ pt.

Made and printed in Great Britain by
Richard Clay (The Chaucer Press), Ltd., Bungay, Suffolk

CHAPTER ONE

'ARE you sure you don't want me to stay, darling?' The rare endearment emphasised Katherine Ashley's concern for her newly widowed daughter. Turning to her husband, she appealed for his support. 'Howard, don't you think she should come home with us?' Then, without waiting for his answer, she spoke again to Elise. 'You shouldn't be alone, tonight—we'll take you home. Howard——'

'But I *want* to be alone, Mother,' Elise said evenly, the calmness of her voice exactly a match for the serenity of her pale face, its purity of line emphasised by the smoothly drawn back style of her fair hair and the limpid green of her eyes, unmarred by any sign of tears.

Her father looked at her, slim and almost fragile-looking in the very plain black dress that somehow seemed to emphasise and heighten her femininity, an impression that was belied by the firm set of her pretty mouth, the determined set of her chin. He was sure she had not shed a tear since the police had called in the middle of the night three days before to inform her that her husband had been the victim of a fatal car crash. He was proud of his daughter, a pride faintly mixed with a dim sense of guilt because he had never really taken the time to know her when she was a child—and she had grown up so quickly and married so young. Now she was a composed young woman of twenty-five, and Katherine, who had always been a somewhat exacting mother, was offering her comfort as to a child.

'Dear——' Katherine's normally austere features soft-

ened as she touched her daughter's arm in persuasion,
'you've been very brave, you don't want to give in now,
and become morbid on your own—come to us for a
while until you get over——'

'I'm quite all right, Mother. I won't go to pieces, I
promise.'

But her green eyes lifted to Howard's face, looking
past her mother, and he thought that he read a slight
flicker of appeal in them.

'Kate!' he said, and his wife turned in astonishment
at the peremptory note in his voice. It was a note which
his numerous employees would have recognised at once,
and jumped to obey, from the newest office boy to the
managers of his branch stores, but Katherine had never
heard it in a remark addressed to her before.

'Howard?' she said, surprised and a little indignant.

'Elise knows what she wants, I think. You can phone
her tomorrow in case she changes her mind. You know
you can come home any time, Elise, and stay as long as
you want.'

'Thank you, Dad.'

He knew she didn't want it at all, and wouldn't come.
And for no reason his mind went back to a time many
years ago when he had been away on one of his frequent business trips, and had brought her back a huge,
elaborate and very expensive doll's cradle. He recalled
her thanking him in just that tone of voice, conveying
both appreciation for the thought that had prompted it,
and a complete indifference to the gift itself. Katherine
had said later that at eleven, Elise was growing a little
old for dolls, and he had felt relieved because then he
understood. Next time he had brought her scented soap
and talcum powder and a manicure set in a leather case,
but he didn't remember that her reaction had been any
different.

He said gruffly, 'Come on, Katherine.'

Obediently she took his arm, but with a faint air of displeasure, and Elise moved forward to accompany them to the door. She presented her cheek for her mother's kiss, and looked a little surprised when her father bent to touch his lips to her smooth, cool skin. He didn't remember when he had ever seen Elise kiss anyone voluntarily, even her husband. For the first time he wondered if she and Peter had been happy. He had always taken it for granted before. At eighteen she had seemed eager enough to marry him, and he and Katherine had been rather relieved, because although Elise was basically a good girl, there had been occasional signs of a latent and disturbing wildness in her. A good steady marriage with a man a few years older than herself had seemed the very thing for her ...

When they had gone, the smooth purr of her father's expensive car receding down the driveway, Elise locked the door and let out a long sigh of luxurious relief. For a few moments she allowed her shoulders to sag, her head to droop forward against a slim hand on her forehead. But when she glanced up and saw herself in the hall mirror looking like that—weary and lost—she straightened up and walked into the roomy L-shaped lounge, looking about her for ashtrays to empty, cushions to straighten, something to occupy her hands and deaden her mind.

It had all been done. Her mother's efficiency, of course, aided by the able Mrs Benton who came in three times a week at her mother's house and had been only too glad to help with the necessary hospitality and subsequent cleaning up today.

The room still smelled faintly of cigarette smoke, and Elise crossed to the big side windows and opened them

up. The day had clouded over late in the afternoon, and a
cold breeze blew the curtains into the room and made
her shiver, but she stood there looking out at the garden
where she had planted a mixture of native and imported
plants five years ago when she and Peter, newly married,
had moved into their brand-new home.

The roses had done well, reds, golds and creams bloom-
ing fulsomely on sturdy, prickled stems. The dainty
Japanese maple in one corner of the neat lawn was a
respectable tree, already ten feet tall. The lacy-leaved
red kowhai too, had been a quick grower. In an angle of
the house a silver tree fern shaded pink and red fuchsias,
and over near the front fence the kauri she had planted
last year was still only a stripling. Peter had teased her
about that. 'In a hundred years' time it might be a
proper tree. Do you plan to be about then?'

'Don't you?' she had asked him, smiling. She couldn't
say, 'Our children might be.' They had stopped talking
about that, last year, or perhaps the year before. She
wasn't sure. But there had been no undercurrent in their
bantering about the kauri. Perhaps a suburban garden on
the outskirts of Auckland wasn't quite the place for a
forest giant that might live a thousand years and attain
a girth of mammoth proportions, but she liked to think
that it would be there after they had gone, perhaps after
the house was gone ...

Elise smiled faintly, and bit her lip, turning away dry-
eyed from the garden and the memories. The curtain
lifted and draped itself over a small side-table, pulling
at a small figurine and lifting it, dragging until the ornament fell harmlessly on to the thick pile of the carpet.

She picked it up and replaced it on the table, and shut
the windows. Instantly the room seemed stuffy and
close, although the cigarette smell had gone. A box of
expensive filter-tips lay open on the table by the door,

and she put out a hand to close it as she passed, her fingers lingering on the tooled leather of the lid, opening it up again, recalling the sharp taste of tobacco smoke, the slow pleasure of drawing it into her mouth and throat ...

Sharply she flicked the lid down again. She had given up smoking years ago. She had not refused Dr Burton's proffered sedatives to give in to the dubious relaxing effects of the insidiously risky cigarette.

No. She would cope, as she always did, without drugs, without crutches of any kind.

She supposed the hollow feeling in her stomach was hunger. It didn't feel like hunger, but since she had forced herself to swallow a cup of coffee and two pieces of toast at breakfast time, she hadn't eaten. There had been plenty of food for the people who invaded the house after the funeral. She had made sure of the sandwiches, the scones, the sherry ... She supposed there would be plenty left in the kitchen, tidily put away by Mrs Benton. Perhaps she should make some tea and have a leftover sandwich.

The sharp buzz of the doorbell interrupted her thoughts. It would be a messenger with flowers, arriving late, or another telegram, she supposed. She didn't want to answer the door. It was supposed to be all over now. They could leave the flowers on the doorstep, bring the telegram tomorrow. Go away.

The bell rang again, with a short, peremptory sound. She waited, standing still, thinking, *go away, go away.*

They didn't. The next peal was prolonged, impatient. Afterwards, there was silence but no sound of retreating steps moving off the tiled porch, down the driveway.

Again the unknown caller pressed the bell, insistent and determined. 'Damn you,' Elise murmured tiredly, without anger, and went unhurriedly to answer it at last.

She opened the door without curiosity, noting as she did so that the light was fading, standing just inside the doorway while her fingers held the edge of the door, her face a cold mask of polite enquiry, her feet placed precisely in their high-heeled black shoes, the plain dress skimming a lovely body that held itself straight and taut so that in stillness she looked almost stiff, nearly angular, although all her movements held a quick grace.

The man who stood facing her was tall, giving her some inches even in her high heels. He wore a suit, but he wore it as though it was, or might have been, worn jeans and a bush shirt. One hand was thrust into a trouser pocket, and the other was leaning on the wall above the bell-push, his thumb poised to ring again. His attitude brought his shoulders hunching forward, so that when she opened the door he seemed to lean over her almost threateningly. The impression was underscored by the expression on his dark face, which was grim. He had an aggressive chin, a stubborn mouth that curved equally easily into cruelty or amusement, straight dark brows over flint-grey eyes, and crisp dark hair that always looked as though he dragged a comb through it impatiently every morning and occasionally remembered to have cut.

He didn't greet her, but he straightened up and looked at her, a comprehensive, almost insolent look, except that there was no deliberate insolence there, just a calm certainly that he had every right to look at her that way and that she knew it.

She should have been angry, because she had never allowed Shard Cortland the rights he claimed, and a long time ago she had made it clear to him that she never would. But she felt no anger, just a distant relief that in fact she could feel nothing at all. It was nice, she discovered, to feel nothing. She wished the numbness could last for the rest of her life.

Then he moved, and she instinctively stepped back, because he was walking into the house as though he had every right there, too, and she knew that it was no use trying to stop him.

He took the door from her hand and pushed it shut behind him and said, 'You're pale. Are you all right?'

'Yes,' she said, and waited. She might have said, 'Please come in,' or 'How kind of you to call,' but with Shard the ordinary courtesies were irrelevant. So were a lot of other ordinary things, when he was around. It had always been like that. She had not seen him since her marriage, but nothing had changed.

At that thought, a faint, faraway warning tingled in her brain somewhere, momentarily stopped her breath. But it passed quickly and when Shard looked round, found the open doorway of the lounge and went through it, she followed him.

He waited for her to sit down, looking at her, but she had the distinct feeling that he had already assessed the room, the paintings on the walls, the thickness of the carpet—and that he was quietly amused by it.

She sat on the sofa, facing him as he stood by an armchair near the fireplace with its gleaming chain-screen. She carefully crossed her ankles and folded her hands in her lap.

He looked at the discreet mahogany fitting built into the corner behind her and said, 'Is that where you keep drinks?'

'Yes.'

Before she could offer him anything, he said, 'I'll get you one.' She sat where she was as she heard him open the cabinet, and when he asked, 'Dry sherry all right?'

she said quietly, 'Yes. Thank you.'

His hand appeared over her shoulder holding a glass, the liquid faintly moving against the sides, and she took it from him, glancing only as high as the sleeve of his jacket as she murmured her thanks. It was a good jacket in fine dark wool, and the expanding watch strap she glimpsed beneath his shirt cuff looked like real gold.

She said, as he came around the sofa, 'Would you turn on the lamp—on the table there. Thank you.'

A pool of light surrounded them, and she wished she had asked him to switch on the central one, a modern chandelier, instead. The shadows in the far corners of the room seemed to draw the sofa and the deep armchair which he had taken, closer together.

She sipped at her sherry, savouring the sharpness against her tongue. 'I didn't know you were in Auckland,' she commented.

'I've only been here a week, this time,' he said. 'I saw the funeral notice in the paper.'

She turned the glass in her hand. There had been a lot of people at the church. Her family and Peter's were both well known in the business community. 'I didn't see you among the mourners,' she said. She was glad she had not seen him. But she should show appreciation of his coming.

Shard said, 'I'm not a mourner.'

Elise stopped turning her glass, the distant warning again stopping her breath for a brief space of time. She said, 'You—weren't at the church?'

There was a short silence before he answered, but she kept her eyes on the sherry that remained in her glass. 'I wasn't at the church. I waited for you—until everyone had gone.'

She glanced up then, surprise getting through the icy indifference that enveloped her. He had been watching the house, waiting until she was alone.

She said, 'My mother wanted to stay with me. Or take me home.'

He didn't answer, but she saw in his eyes that he had known she would choose solitude. That he had only to wait.

With a faint stirring of anger, she said, 'I wanted to be alone.'

A very slight quirk at the corner of his mouth acknowledged the hint, but he didn't take it.

Elise quelled her anger without effort and said, 'It was kind of you to come.'

Shard's eyes narrowed. 'I'm not kind—you know it.'

'It's six years,' she shrugged. 'You might have changed.'

'I haven't.'

He was watching her, waiting for a reaction that she wouldn't give. Once she would have found a painful pleasure in withholding it. Now there wasn't even that. She was glad of her own indifference.

She said, 'You haven't poured a drink for yourself. Please——'

'I don't want one.' Shard was relaxed in the deep leather chair, his hands lying along the arms. They were strong hands with long fingers and blunt, short-cut nails. 'Would you like another?' he asked.

'No, thank you.' There was still an inch of golden-brown liquid in her glass, but with her hand curved about it he couldn't see that.

'Has it been very bad?' he asked abruptly.

'It's been—a nightmare,' she said bleakly. Then she added, 'But I'm very lucky. People have been wonderful. And my family—they've helped me a lot.'

'Yes.' It came out a flat, expressionless monosyllable. At one time it might have needled her, made her flare up at him, but now she glanced at him once, her eyes coolly blank, and lifted her glass to finish her drink and sit politely waiting for him to take his leave.

He didn't. He rose and took the glass from her and put it on the table beside the lamp. Then he turned to face her again and unexpectedly put his hand under her chin, lifting her face to the light. His fingers were warm and hard and when she made an involuntary movement of escape, they tightened and hurt her.

She didn't complain, and her eyes held no particular resentment as they met the cold blaze of his.

He released her and said, 'Have they been feeding you tranquillisers?'

'No. The doctor gave me a sedative the first night, but I've refused everything since.'

'What about food?'

'I was just about to get myself something when you rang.'

Shard swung away from her and left the room, and she heard him opening doors until he found the kitchen. She should go and tell him she could manage, he wasn't needed—or wanted. But she suddenly felt tired, and it had never been any good telling Shard anything ... She would only exhaust herself and get nowhere. Elise leaned her head back against the sofa and closed her eyes.

The carpet muffled his footsteps when he came back, but she heard him put down the tray he had found on the table beside her, and opened her eyes. He had toasted some of the sandwiches and heated some slices of pizza pie, and made a pot of tea.

She said, 'I can't eat all that.'

'I'm hungry, too,' Shard told her, and began pouring tea into two cups. 'Here, you look as though you need something warm.'

She ate some sandwiches, refused the pie, and drank two cups of tea, and the empty feeling receded.

Shard took the tray back to the kitchen when she had finished, and she heard him rattling cups and plates as he washed up. She smiled faintly. She had never thought of Shard as domesticated. Maybe the years had tamed him a little, after all.

He came back into the room and she realised how far out she had been in thinking that. She stood up, hinting that he should consider his visit over. She started to thank him for what he had done, and was cut short. 'I'm not going yet, and you don't need to thank me. Sit down.'

When she didn't, he came to her and grasped her arms, not roughly but with purpose, and pushed her back on to the sofa. Then he sat beside her, and she was dismayed to find life trickling back into her nerves, her skin, awareness like pain bringing her back to full life again, like the blood surging back into numbed limbs, hurting that way.

She breathed carefully, trying to hold on to the blessed numbness, the restful indifference that had protected her before. She folded her hand as before and kept her eyes fixed on them, kept her fingers relaxed, tranquil-looking.

He said, 'You haven't cried, have you?'

Elise didn't answer him. There was no need, because he knew the answer; the way he asked the question told her that.

He said, with an edge of roughness in his deep voice, 'When you opened the door, you looked the picture of a grieving widow. But you haven't cried for him. What kind of marriage was it, Elise?'

She looked up then, her eyes meeting his steadily. 'It was a good marriage. I made him happy.' She saw the flicker of something in his face and added, 'We were very happy—both of us.'

'Were you.' The flat sounds indicated nothing, not disbelief, certainly not a question. 'Then why don't you grieve?'

'I *am* grieving!' She said it with little emphasis and only a hint of defiance.

'Deep inside?' he said, his voice derisive. 'With a stiff upper lip, of course. I thought marriage might have changed you. But you're still afraid of emotion, aren't you?'

'I'm not *afraid*, and I never was. I just don't think it's necessary to give in to it. Peter wouldn't have wanted me to indulge in floods of tears at his funeral.'

'Are you saving them for a suitable time?'

'You're being deliberately offensive!' she snapped, standing up. 'I think you'd better go.'

He stood, but stayed facing her. 'So that you can go and shed a few genteel tears in the privacy of your bedroom?'

'*Go away!*'

She saw in his eyes that this was what he had wanted —to make her angry. She didn't understand why, but she felt dimly that he meant to hurt her. 'Why did you come?' she asked him, trying to control her anger. 'To gloat? Did you want to see me cry? Is that it?'

He said, 'I want to see you cry.'

After all these years he had the power to hurt her as no one else ever had, except perhaps her father, long ago. And he had never known of his power. But Shard knew. Shard had always known.

Elise turned away from the knowledge in his eyes, her hand blindly closing over a hardness on the table nearby —a brass vase from Benares. Her fingers grasped the metal, feeling it cold against her flesh, and behind her Shard said, 'Go on, Elise, throw it at me.'

She fought down the urge to do it, the terrible, primitive urge to hurl it at his dark head and watch blood wipe the smile from his face, the mockery from his eyes.

She took her fingers from the vase and laid them flat against the table. 'I hate you, Shard,' she muttered.

'Of course. You'd have to—to go on living with Peter.'

Suddenly the fury flooded up, and she turned on him, her hands rigid at her sides to stop herself hitting out at him in a blind, undignified rage. 'How *dare* you!' she cried. 'You're not even fit to say his name—how *dare* you sneer at him!'

'I dare,' he said. 'And you know why.' He stepped closer to her, so that she backed up against the table behind her. 'What was it like, Elise? Tell me how it was, being married to Peter——'

She screamed at him, '*Shut up!*' Her hands formed into fists and beat against his shoulders, and when he caught her wrists she tried to twist away. He twisted her wrist in his hand until he could see her face and the tears escaping from her closed eyelids, her lips clamped tightly against the anguish that shook her. Then he pulled her roughly into his arms and held her until she stopped struggling and lay helplessly sobbing against his chest.

She cried for a long time, and Shard held her there, not sitting down but supporting her weight with his feet spread apart, and his arm against her waist, his other hand stroking her shoulders, her back and her hair. He pulled the pins from the knot at her nape and let them fall on the floor, smoothing her hair back from her hot forehead as the sobs lessened and she stayed quiet against him, her hands pressed to his shirt where his jacket had fallen open.

His hand closed on her shoulder and stayed there until she moved, pushing away, and then he handed her his handkerchief and watched as she turned her back on him to use it. She pushed her hair back and squared her shoulders and then gave back his handkerchief, neatly folded but damp. She didn't thank him.

He put the handkerchief back in his pocket, still watching her.

She demanded, 'Satisfied?'

'No.'

She closed her eyes. 'You wanted to see me cry, now you've seen it. What more do you want?'

'You.'

Her eyes flew open. Her tears had blurred the green of them. They looked dark and confused. Her voice husky, she said, 'You have a colossal nerve. I don't think there's another man on this earth who would have the incredible bad taste to say that to a woman on the day of her husband's funeral.'

'I wasn't propositioning you, and you know it. I lay no claim to good taste, Elise, but I know you're not ready for that yet.'

She said, 'I still hate you, Shard.'

'I know—more than ever since you cried on my shoulder. You'll get over it, just as you'll get over your grief for Peter. I can't be the first one to tell you that.'

'No. For once you're less than original.'

'You're young,' they had said, and she had heard the unspoken implication that they were too tactful to voice.

But Shard wasn't tactful. 'You're young,' he said, consciously echoing the well-meaning cliché. 'You're beautiful and you'll marry again. Isn't that what they said?'

'Not to my face.'

'Well, I'm saying it to your face. And I'll say this too. Next time it's going to be me. You won't run from me again.'

Elise wished she could laugh in his arrogant face. She looked at the hardness about his mouth and the cold glitter of his eyes and saw no desire and no tenderness, only a taut air of purpose.

'You're mad!' she exclaimed. 'I'll never marry you. Not if you were the last man on earth——'

'I'm the *only* man on earth—for you,' he said.

'It's true you haven't changed. You're as conceited as ever.'

He shrugged. 'If that's what you want to call it. I have to go back to Wellington tomorrow, but I'll be here again in two weeks or so. Will you still be here?'

'I have no idea,' she said coldly.

'I'll find you,' said Shard. He took a card from his pocket and laid it on the table beside the lamp. 'If you want to contact me, this has phone numbers in Auckland and Wellington on it,' he said. 'Goodnight, Elise.'

He walked out, evidently not expecting her to escort him to the door, and she didn't.

She stood looking at the small oblong of cardboard long after his footsteps had receded down the driveway. Then she picked it up and found an ashtray and a box of matches, and carefully burned it to a few blackened wisps of ash.

CHAPTER TWO

ELISE slept well, the first time since Peter's death. In the morning she woke feeling as though a fog had lifted. There was pain, for the nightmare had become stark and uncompromising reality, but the helplessness of the nightmare was gone, too. She made herself eat breakfast and rang her mother to ask her to help sort Peter's clothes for giving away to one of her mother's charities. Then she phoned a real estate agency.

By five o'clock that night the house was listed at the agency for sale, all Peter's personal belongings had been despached to his mother or a charity, except a few things Elise kept for herself, and she had arranged to lease a beach cottage in a quiet part of the Bay of Plenty for a month, starting at the end of the week.

'Alone?' her mother queried with an air of disapproval.

'Yes, mother, alone.'

'Now, Elise, you're not going to brood, are you? Don't you think a week might be enough?'

'If it is, I'll come back in a week. I'm not obliged to stay the entire month.'

But she knew she would stay if it killed her. She wasn't coming back to Auckland until Shard Cortland had given up looking for her and accepted that she meant it when she said she would never marry him.

'But what will you do?' her mother asked sharply.

'Brush up on my drawing,' Elise answered. 'I may be looking for a job when I get back.'

'Well, I'm sure Peter will have left you very comfortably off,' said Katherine. 'But I suppose you'll need an interest ...'

Elise was surprised at the lack of opposition to the suggestion of a job. Her mother had backed up Peter's opposition to her working when they were married. She had taken an art course after leaving school, and illustrated a children's book for a friend, but both Peter and her mother had expressed unease at her making a career of it.

'I think it's very clever of you, darling,' Peter said kindly. 'But just keep it occasional, will you? I don't want you getting in a flap over meeting deadlines and that sort of thing. But if the odd illustrating job makes you happy and doesn't put too great a strain on you, well, that just fine.'

Peter never forbade her anything or actively disapproved. He just made it clear that everything was secondary to his business and the happiness of their marriage. Which was as it should be, she told herself. He was always careful to keep her informed about his work, and include her in the social side of it.

Her mother was more forthright. 'Peter is a young man still making his way, and he needs a wife who can support him, not one trying to make her own career. I know it's fashionable now for both husband and wife to work, but it's the men with a wife behind them who are successful, you'll see. Marriage needs to be worked at, and Peter needs a good hostess who isn't too concerned with her own affairs to take an active interest in his business.'

Elise knew that marriage needed to be worked at. She could see that Peter was taking pains to fit her into his busy life, and she felt that it was up to her to fill the niche that he made for her. She worked at her marriage, and it was a success. So was Peter's business. Her mother approved, and frequently pointed out marriages that were going on the rocks because the careers of the husband and wife conflicted, or they had ceased to have time for each other. Elise didn't point out those she knew of which broke up even though the wife had no career of her own.

'Will you be home tonight?' her mother enquired, and not waiting for an answer, because where would Elise be going? she went on, 'Gary and Della would like to come round and spend the evening with you. They fly back to Wellington tomorrow.'

Her brother and his wife had stayed with her parents for a few days while they attended the funeral, and Elise knew that her mother had probably coerced them into spending some time with her tonight. Della was pregnant and had not come to the cemetery after the church service. Gary had taken her back to his parents' house instead. The thought of death frightened Della, who was a timid person inclined to 'nerves', and Elise was sure that it was a toss-up with her if the more agonising evening would be to spend time with a newly bereaved sister-in-law, or a glacially polite mother-in-law, who made it plain she was neglecting a glaringly plain duty of courtesy.

Elise made a determined effort to be cheerful that evening for Della's sake, helping to avoid any mention of Peter's name, and seeing them off with a peculiar feeling that they had been pretending for several hours that her husband had never existed.

It wasn't until she had undressed and got into bed that she identified the source of the vague feeling of relief she admitted when they had gone. It was not simply because the evening had gone off without any notable awkward pauses, or because Della had not been forced to acknowledge Peter's death. It was because they had not mentioned the name of Shard Cortland.

Gary had brought Shard into her life, when she was eighteen and engaged to Peter Westwood.

Peter was everything a girl could possibly want in a husband. He had looks and charm and was already established as a partner in a well-known accountancy firm, with good connections in the business world. His family had wealth and a good name, and both their families aided and abetted the romance with the greatest goodwill. He was quite a lot older than Elise, over thirty, but still a young man, and Elise's friends thought that more than twelve years' difference in age only added to his undeniable glamour.

When he showed an interest in Elise, she was flattered, and for the first time she set out to make a man fall in love with her. It had been surprisingly easy, and she didn't think Peter ever knew that it was she who chose the time and the place the first time he kissed her. It was a satisfying kiss and she enjoyed it. He was more experienced than the boys she had kissed before, and he wasn't clumsy or over-eager, and it rather amused her that he seemed to be careful not to frighten her.

He said ruefully as he let her go, 'I shouldn't have done that.'

'Why ever not?' she asked, astonished.

'I'm a lot older than you are.'

Elise laughed, 'I've been kissed before,' and was gratified by the quick flash of jealousy in his eyes.

It wasn't hard to persuade herself that she was in love with Peter, and when he asked her to marry him she had no hesitation about accepting him.

'I told your father I'm willing to wait until you're twenty,' he said. 'But I want my ring on your finger.'

She looked up into his face and laughed. 'You mean you asked my father's permission? How old-fashioned of you, darling!'

He smiled, his blue eyes gentle as he moved a strand of fair hair from his sleeve where she leaned her head against the curve of his arm. 'My darling, you're so young, I felt I should. I wanted to make the wedding sooner—you're nearly nineteen, aren't you? But your father is right. We'll wait.'

'More than a year?' she asked slowly.

'As soon as you're legally of age,' he said, his voice husky. 'Please.'

Elise touched his cheek with her hand, and slid her fingers into his beautifully cut brown hair. Peter was always immaculately groomed, and she enjoyed seeing him slightly tousled and a little less controlled than usual after kissing her. She felt meltingly fond of him, and was suddenly aware of a sense of responsibility for this man who was putting his life into her careless young hands.

'Yes, Peter,' she said. 'We can be married on my birthday, if you like.'

'Would you like it?' His voice was urgent, his eyes alight with controlled passion.

'Yes,' she said, her lips inviting his. 'Yes, please, Peter.'

She met his kiss with her arms wound about his neck, and he held her more closely than ever before, so that in the end she protested that he was hurting her.

'I'm sorry, my darling,' he said as he let her go. '*I love you so much!*' he added, his hand almost crushing hers. 'I wish you were older—no, I don't. I love you just as you are.'

'You mean you wish I was more experienced, don't you? So that you wouldn't feel obliged to wait for the wedding.'

'No!' But his face flushed darkly, and she knew something like that had been in his mind.

She looked at him sideways, her mouth curving into a provocative smile. 'Supposing I said you don't have to?'

Peter looked at her with no answering smile. 'You don't mean that, Elise,' he said curtly, the tone a reprimand.

No, she had not meant it. She had wanted to see his reaction, and he had scolded her like a child. Well, she supposed she deserved it.

'I was teasing,' she explained, her cheeks flushing.

'Yes. I won't be teased, Elise. You musn't do it.'

But she did, only more subtly. She teased him because she didn't like that fast switch from an adoring lover to a stern mentor. She punished him by being a little aloof, elusive. And friendly with other men. She didn't flirt, just listened and smiled and seemed so interested and absorbed in what they were telling her that she failed to notice Peter's vain attempts to detach her.

She succeeded in making him angry, then fell into his arms, crying contritely, 'But darling, I didn't mean it like that! You told me not to tease, and I thought—I thought you meant not to—to tempt you!'

It worked beautifully. He pulled her close and apologised in a shaken voice, his lips against her skin, telling her she was the sweetest thing on earth and he was a brute, that he adored her.

Genuinely contrite and feeling guilty, Elise was touched enough to forget to feel triumph at her victory. Peter was really far too good for her, she knew. She would try her best to live up to his picture of her. Because she loved him and he deserved the best.

She only tested him once after that. Her father had given her a car for her eighteenth birthday, over her mother's protest. It was a sporty little low-slung convertible, a rich girl's car and one of two things she had ever asked him for. The first had been a pony, when she was twelve, and she had insisted on a mount that everyone considered too fast and too frisky for a learner. The pony threw her, not once but several times, but she got up and remounted until she learned to ride and to make the pony mind her. It was the speed that had attracted her, the sense of freedom in galloping miles over rolling farmland with her hair streaming behind her and the wind in the pony's mane whipping it back against her face as she bent over his straining neck. She never went to pony club like the other girls of her age, and although her mother had insisted on her having a hard hat, she would pull it off after the first few minutes, hang it on a fence-post to be fetched later, and then let the pony have his head.

When she got the car she was issued with a speeding ticket within the first week. Her mother was horrified and her father stern.

'If it happens again, I'll sell the car, Elise,' he warned.

'It's in my name, Dad,' she said calmly. 'You can't.'

'You'll find out what I can do, young lady,' he said grimly. 'You're still a minor. I'm trying to treat you like an adult, Elise, so please try to act like one, and don't upset your mother like this again.'

She didn't think threatening to sell the car was treating her like an adult, but she didn't say so, because her father was visibly thawing, and she could see that contrition was a more useful attitude at the moment than defiance. Except for odd flashes of stubborn independence which alarmed her mother and puzzled her father, she had never been a rebellious teenager.

Her father paid the fine, and she never got another ticket. She found some winding back roads in the hills among the farms and patches of bush south of Auckland and would sometimes take the car out there and push down the accelerator until she seemed about to fly off the edges of the curves into the space below between the blue, cloud-hung sky and the neatly dissected fields in the valley that she glimpsed between the pungas, king-ferns and kahikatea, puriri and totara that lined the road.

Twice she took young men with her. They were in love with her and she wanted to know if she could be in love with them. She took them up a particularly steep hill over a narrow road with hairpin curves, and she pushed the little car to its limit, her eyes on the bumpy grey metal of the road, littered with loose stones, because these quiet back roads were not tarsealed. And she saw the young men brace their legs and clench their hands, and heard their pent breath escaping when she braked at the top of the hill and got out to look down at the glimpses of curving road between the trees behind them, and the grey dust of their progress slowly drifting and settling on the leaves. Neither of them protested or asked her to slow down, and she said nothing about the clenched fists and the braced thighs. One of them kissed her there at the top of the hill, and she knew that he thought she expected it. But she never went out with either of them again.

She took Peter on the same drive one fine evening soon after their engagement was announced. They seemed to have been endlessly tied ever since to going to parties and social functions together to receive the congratulations of their mutual friends and meet each other's. Her mother had plans for a big party which was to take place the following Saturday, but for this one evening they were free, after spending the afternoon at the races at Ellerslie. It was a dress-up affair, and Peter had shown his appreciation of Elise's new dress which she had had made for the occasion. She had chosen a sophisticated style to make her look older, in gun-metal blue silk, and put up her hair under an elegant matching turban. Her shoes were very high-heeled.

At the end of the day her feet hurt, and after an early dinner at her home she went to her room and changed into jeans and a loose tee-shirt, let down her hair and sauntered back to the living room where Peter was being politely attentive and just a very little deferential to her father.

'Peter?' she said.

Both men smiled at her, and she perched on the arm of her fiancé's chair, loosened his tie with an intimate little gesture, and said, 'Let's go for a drive. In my car.'

Peter looked to her father, who smiled with conscious indulgence and said, 'Go ahead. I'm sure you two would like to be alone for a change.'

Elise drove at a decorous pace until they left the motorway, then gradually increased her speed. Peter had taken off his jacket and tie and with the top button of his shirt undone he looked young and dashingly hand-some, the breeze whipping his hair into disorder. He raised his hand to it a few times, brushing it down, but then gave up, and leaned back against the seat, his arm behind her, just touching her shoulders, his hand grip-ping the seat back just by her.

She opened up as they reached the bottom of the hill, swinging the wheel competently as they skidded round corners, checking a slide expertly as the wheels neared the edge of the metal. They were going very fast, and she glanced at Peter's hand on his knee, loose and relaxed, and a small smile touched her mouth. They came out of a corner and she accelerated into the next one, and he turned his head so that his lips were close to her ear and said quietly, 'Stop showing off, Elise.'

Her foot eased off the pedal, and they swept decorously around the remaining curves and glided to a gentle halt at the brow of the hill.

She looked at him with apology in her smile, and he smiled back at her indulgently. 'You silly child!' he said. His hand moved to her shoulder and he pulled her to him and kissed her, very gently. She moved closer to him and he lifted his head and broke the kiss, taking her hand and holding it in his, looking at his ring on her finger. It was a large diamond flanked by two smaller ones, and it was lovely and had cost a lot of money. Peter had said he could afford it, and besides, it could be looked on as an investment.

Elise knew why he had drawn away, and was suddenly awed by the power she wielded over him. Just now he was the masterful, protective older lover, but she could change that whenever she cared to. She knew she could have made him beg, and the thought shocked her. She felt wicked and unworthy of his love. She thought she loved him very much and would never hurt him.

She moved her hand in his to clasp his fingers in hers, and when he looked up at her, she whispered, 'I love you.'

She felt his fingers tighten, and he moved until his lips just touched her forehead, keeping them there for several seconds, almost like an act of homage. Then he kissed her mouth very briefly and said, 'We'd better get back. Your father will be wondering where we are.'

'Oh, he won't worry,' she assured him. 'He trusts you. Of course, he may not trust *me*!'

'Don't be silly, my dear,' he said mildly. She smiled as she started the engine. The homage was gone, but she knew she could call it up whenever she wanted to. She was going to enjoy being married to Peter. They would be very happy.

*

She hadn't met Shard Cortland then.

Gary brought him home for the Christmas break. Gary was at university then, and during the long Christmas holiday he had taken a job in Te Puke, labouring on a building site. His mother didn't like it very much, but his father approved wholeheartedly. Of course, he didn't need to work his way through university, but it wouldn't do him any harm to learn what hard work was, Howard believed.

When he said he would like to bring a friend home for Christmas, a friend with no family of his own, Katherine assumed he meant a fellow-student. She felt very sorry for a young man who had no family, especially at Christmas time. Their own Christmas was always very much a family affair. It was a tradition that her sister and brother-in-law, who were childless, spent Christmas day with the Ashleys, and Howard's elderly father would be collected from the exclusive nursing home where he now lived, to join them for Christmas dinner.

'And Gary is bringing a friend,' she told them all complacently. She was a very efficient hostess, and liked having guests. The children had both been encouraged to bring their friends home all their lives, and she flattered herself that she had always made them welcome, though of course there had been mistakes—children were not always discriminating in their friendships ...

Elise had soon learned which friends to bring home and which to keep out of her mother's way. Her mother never said a word to her directly, but she had a way of asking questions which set some of the children wriggling with half-understood embarrassment, and Elise didn't like to see her friends suffer. 'Where do you live, dear?' and 'What does your father do?' seemed innocuous enough, and she always smiled as she nodded at the answer and said, 'I see,' but to some answers there seemed an invisible reaction of distaste, while others elicited a smile of extra warmth.

Gary, who had a peculiar quality of innocence, and a ready sympathy for any misfortune, continued to bring home 'unsuitable' companions of all kinds until he passed primary school age and was sent to an exclusive college for boys, when the problem virtually resolved itself. The only boys he met there were roughly from the same social stratum as his own family, and it was to be assumed by the time he reached university a natural quality of discrimination would have asserted itself, Katherine thought.

She expected a respectable young student, perhaps a little diffident, almost certainly grateful for being taken into the Ashley family circle over the ten-day Christmas break. She was quite unprepared for Shard.

Elise was unprepared, too. She had turned nineteen at the beginning of December and reminded Peter that meant it was exactly a year to their wedding day. He needed no reminding, he said, kissing her cheek softly as he presented her with his gift—a finely wrought gold pendant with two small diamonds worked into the pattern.

'Next year it will be a wedding ring,' he told her.

'Yes,' she said, lifting her mouth for his kiss.

On Christmas Eve he came round to put his gifts for her family under the big tree in the lounge. There were neighbours there who had dropped in for a pre-Christmas sherry—another Ashley tradition, and Howard had invited two of his branch managers and their wives to join them, too.

There was quite a crowd in the lounge when Gary arrived, and Elise, busy with Peter arranging his parcels, having briefly helped her mother introduce him to the other guests, didn't realise that her brother had arrived

until she heard her father's voice behind her say to someone, 'And this is my son.'

She turned with a surprised smile on her face, looking
for Gary, and her glance collided with a pair of glinting
grey eyes that stopped hers and held them with a sudden
blaze of interest.

She wasn't aware that her own eyes had widened and
darkened with a shock that was like recognition, although she knew she had never met the man before. And
then he turned away to acknowledge an introduction
and she was left staring at the back of an unruly dark
head, and broad shoulders in a faded denim shirt, with
a small tear on the back.

Peter turned and said, 'Oh, Gary's here.'

'Yes,' said Elise. Any other time she would have run to
greet her brother, but now she needed time to collect herself.

When he brought Shard over and introduced them,
she kept her eyes on Gary at first, according Shard the
briefest glance with her smiling 'Hello,' and not offering
her hand.

She felt his gaze on her, and as Gary said, 'And this is
the guy who's brave enough to marry my sister, Peter
Westwood,' she lifted her eyes to his face. She saw a
brief blankness, and that he was still looking at her, and
then he moved his gaze to Peter's face and studied it
with apparent interest, slowly putting out his hand to
meet the one extended to him.

She heard him say, 'You're a lucky man, Peter Westwood,' and thought that his voice matched his looks,
dark and deep and with an underlying hardness. Peter's
arm was casually about her shoulders and he agreed,
'Yes, I am.'

Shard's mouth moved in a way that was not quite a
smile. He knew he was being gently warned off. His eyes

slid to hers again, and she knew she must have misunder-
stood what was in them, because it looked for all the
world like accusation ...

On Christmas Day they all slept late, having attended
church at midnight. She had heard Gary telling Shard in
low tones that there was no need for him to attend if he
preferred not to. She hadn't caught his reply, but he
came, still dressed in jeans and the torn shirt. Gary was
similarly dressed, though his clothes were newer and
less shabby. Katherine's mouth tightened when she saw
the two of them, but she said nothing.

Katherine had bought and wrapped a present for Gary's
friend. They unwrapped the parcels under the tree before
lunch, after Peter had arrived, and Shard removed the
red and green paper from the parcel Gary handed him,
then read the card which said it was from the family
and said formally to Katherine, 'Thank you very much,
Mrs Ashley. You're very kind.'

Elise glanced at the silk of the dark, beautifully discreet tie and the matching nylon socks, and wondered if
he would ever wear them.

He sat holding the tie and the socks while everyone else
unwrapped parcels and traded thanks. He had brought
no presents for anyone, and he neither apologised nor
explained. It wasn't expected, of course, but most people
would have felt obliged to justify the omission. Shard
evidently didn't. He merely sat looking interested and
unembarrassed.

Before lunch, which was always taken very formally
on Christmas Day, as an afternoon dinner, Katherine,
who was wearing a very elegant housecoat, said pointedly, 'Well, I think it's time to change. Gary, you won't
wear those jeans to the table, will you? Aunt Evelyn
and Uncle Richard—not to mention your grandfather—

will expect the courtesy of a suit, I think.'

'That's a bit outdated, Mother—it's too hot for a suit.'

'Well, at least a shirt and tie, Gary. I do expect a reasonable standard of dress at my table.'

Gary flushed, and Shard rose easily to his feet. 'I think your son is trying to spare my feelings, Mrs Ashley,' he said calmly. 'I think he's seen my—wardrobe, such as it is, and knows I don't have anything but denims and bush shirts. Maybe he might be able to lend me a shirt that won't disgrace your table, and might do justice to this very nice tie you've given me.'

Katherine smiled tightly. 'I beg your pardon, Mr Cortland, I didn't mean to embarrass you——' Although Elise had a sudden conviction that she had suspected this and had intended nothing else.

'I'm not embarrassed, Mrs Ashley,' he said, and Elise saw that he was telling the truth, and also that her mother was angry at his lack of discomfiture, perhaps also at the suggestion that Gary should lend him clothes. 'And the name's Shard, Mrs Ashley. Please.'

He smiled gently, and Elise saw the colour rise under her mother's careful make-up and felt a swift shaft of antagonism for the insolent stranger. As he followed Gary from the room, she checked herself, thinking, *but he was perfectly polite*! Yet she knew that her mother had felt she had been caught out in a discourtesy, and rebuked for it, and that her mother was not imagining things.

He came to the table in a blue shirt of Gary's that strained at the buttons a little, and Elise was sure the one under the knot of the new tie was undone; he was wearing a pair of dark trousers that Elise realised belonged to her father. They were long enough for him, which Gary's would not have been, but a little loose at the waist. He should have looked awkward and a little ridiculous. She realised she had hoped that he would look ridiculous—just slightly. But he looked instead as though he was still wearing the denims and his torn shirt. And as though he knew it and he didn't care.

He ate the traditional roast turkey with green peas and new potatoes with the rest of them, and had two helpings of the plum pudding floating in cream. He answered when spoken to and seemed to be watching them all with an alert, interested gaze. Elise saw him listening to one of her grandfather's stories, his dark head bent to hear the old man's words, and wondered if he could possibly be as relaxed as he looked.

After dinner they sat on the wide paved terrace between the house and the swimming pool, drinking coffee or wine and cracking nuts. Peter and Gary used the nut-crackers, filling a saucer and passing the sweet kernels to the women, while Shard sat on the shallow step near Elise's lounging chair with a handful of whole nuts, cracking them between his hands.

She was watching his hands when he looked up and caught her gaze, and she gave him a contemptuous little smile and turned away.

She knew he had stood up and when he stopped before her and his shadow fell across her chair, she looked up, a half-smile of enquiry on her face.

He was extending his hand to her, half a dozen shelled nuts lying in the curve of his palm. Elise was about to shake her head, give him a cool 'No, thanks,' when he moved and tipped them into her lap, on the silky fabric of her dress. The contempt on his face was a mirror of the look she had given him, but more openly insulting.

Then he moved away and she saw Gary look up and smile and call him over.

Elise sat with the nuts in her closed hand, then got up

abruptly and walked along the side of the pool to the neatly trimmed shrubs that screened the other end from the wind. She dropped the nuts into the soft earth under an azalea and ground the flimsy sole of her sandal down on to them until they disappeared.

As she heard footsteps behind her she whirled and found Peter looking at her quizzically. 'Did I startle you?' he asked.

'It's all right.'

'You look hot, darling. What about a swim?'

'That would be lovely. You'll come in, too, won't you?'

'Yes, I'd like to cool off.'

He put his arm about her waist and she moved her hand to his shoulder and said, 'Kiss me, Peter.'

He glanced towards the imperfect screen of the azalea and smiled down at her. 'That's an invitation that's hard to resist!'

She knew they could be seen from the terrace if any-one was looking in their direction. Not perfectly, but well enough for what they were doing to be unmistak-able.

Perhaps it was because he knew it, too, that Peter's kiss seemed less satisfactory than usual. But his face was flushed when he let her go and said, as he turned her firmly, 'Now I *really* need to cool off!'

She laughed and slipped her arm about his waist as they strolled back to the terrace. Shard had his back to them, he was standing with one arm leaning on a pole that supported the shaded part of the terrace, talking to Gary and Uncle Richard.

Aunt Evelyn saw them coming up the steps and she laughed and said coyly, 'Here come the lovebirds!'

Shard didn't move, but she saw the sudden tautening of the folds in the blue shirt, a slight lifting of the dark head, and she knew that he had been watching.

She swam with Peter, and later some of the others joined them. But Shard didn't swim. He spent most of the afternoon talking to Mr Ashley senior, who looked very animated, as though he was enjoying himself hugely. Usually he nodded off in a quiet corner after Christmas dinner, until it was time for his son to take him back to the rest home.

When Elise left the pool and dressed again, they were still talking, and that annoyed her, because she liked to have a chat to her grandfather and she didn't want to go near Shard Cortland.

But her grandfather beckoned her and although she saw Shard make a move at her approach, the old man caught at his arm and made him sit down again.

'This is a very interesting young man,' he told her. 'We've been having quite a chat.'

She said politely, 'Really? I believe Mr Cortland is in the building trade.'

Shard looked across at her and said, 'Actually, I'm unemployed.' Elise said, 'Really?' with distant politeness again, and wondered what inflection he had used that made his words feel like a blow against her cheek.

'You'll come right, young feller,' her grandfather said confidently. 'You've got what it takes.' He turned to Elise. 'And your young man. Got yourself engaged, haven't you? What's he like?'

She hesitated, conscious of Shard's mocking, interested glance a yard away.

He said, 'She doesn't want to talk about him in front of me, Mr Ashley. I'll leave you.'

This time her grandfather didn't protest, and when he repeated the question, she laughed and said, 'Talk to him yourself. I'll call him.' She had wanted Shard to go away. Now she was annoyed because he had left so readily, as

though he wanted her company even less than she
wanted his.

It was hot in the night, humid and sticky, and she didn't
sleep. Early in the morning, when it was barely light, she
got up and put on a skimpy black bikini and went out
to the pool. She slipped into the cool water and did a
fast crawl to the other end, and then turned to backstroke
to the starting point. The water made her feel alive and
the chill soon receded. She floated a while, then swam
to the deep end and climbed on to the small diving board
erected there. She pushed her wet hair away from her
shoulders. The house looked blind and sleepy. Elise was
the only early riser in the family; everyone else slept
late on holidays.

Slowly she moved her arms forward, eyes closed, then
raised them above her head, her body taut, streaming
with droplets of water. She held her head straight and
opened her eyes—and looked straight at Shard Cortland,
standing at the other end of the pool, dressed in faded
jeans and nothing else but a folded towel slung over one
shoulder.

He stood with his feet planted slightly apart, his
thumbs hooked in the belt of the blue denim pants. And
he looked at her. He looked at her as if she was standing
there, her body poised, arms upstretched, just so that he
could look at her. As though she was flaunting her body
before him, as the old-fashioned phrase had it.

She moved, just a second late, rising on her toes and
bending her knees, feeling the spring of the board as it
lifted her, and her body arced into the air and de-
scended in a graceful curve into the water.

Elise surfaced and swam to the side, and as she found
the smooth tiles, a hand took her wrist and strong fingers

hauled her out. She pushed the wet hair from her eyes and said, 'Thank you.'

He said, 'Beautiful.'

'Thank you,' she said again, coolly. 'I had a very good swimming coach at school. I got a medal for diving.'

She turned away from him to walk along the side of the pool. She hadn't looked at him.

He caught at her hair, tugging the wet strands, and said, 'I didn't mean the dive.'

Elise turned on him, anger blazing in her green eyes. 'Let me go!'

His mouth moved in mockery. 'Sure.' His hand slid down the strand of hair he held, that her movement had brought to the front. The hard knuckles grazed the skin of her shoulder, her breast, and then she was free.

She stepped back and moved past him to pick up her towel and went on to the house. When she turned to the door he was unzipping his trousers, and her breath choked her throat. Shard pulled them off and he had dark swim shorts underneath. He dived into the water with a beautiful clean movement that left hardly a ripple behind. She closed the door before he surfaced.

The day after Boxing Day the shops were open. Shard went out in the afternoon and came back with a huge sheaf of flowers for Katherine and wearing a new shirt made of Chinese natural silk with an expensive look, and a beautifully fitting casual suit that might have been made for him—and by an excellent tailor at that.

He threw the jacket down on the back of a chair as though it was one of his frayed denim outfits worn on the building site, and Elise saw her mother glance at the label and grow suddenly rigid.

'You look very smart, Shard,' said Katherine with condescension. Assuming a look of embarrassed concern,

she added, 'I hope you haven't been spending your savings with the idea of having to live up to our standards.
I'm afraid I was very tactless on Christmas Day—and
Gary tells me that since the building you were both
working on is finished, you're—well, out of work.'

'Don't worry, Mrs Ashley.' Shard smiled, without ran-
cour. 'I needed new clothes, that's all. As I'm sure you
would agree. And I still have some savings left. Though
it's true I haven't a job.'

'Well, I'm sure you'll find something,' Katherine said
vaguely, adding, 'Meantime, I'm very glad Gary brought
you here.'

Elise caught her breath, but Shard was still smiling,
apparently unconcerned. No, more than unconcerned,
Elise decided. He was positively enjoying himself.

He sat in the chair on which he had thrown his new
jacket, apparently careless that his shoulder might crush
it, and she saw that his shoes were new, too, but already
the soles were well scuffed and the uppers dusty. The
crease in the trousers was still sharp and she wondered
how he managed in patently brand new clothes to look
as though he had been wearing them for years, so comfortably did they conform to his body.

On New Year's Eve the Ashleys had a party. Peter and
his parents were there, and a mixture of generations,
Gary's and Elise's friends and friends of their parents.

There was a barbecue on the terrace with swimming
and music to dance to for the young people. Elise was
surprised when her girl friends, surveying the available
men, demanded introductions to Gary's friend.

'You lucky *thing*!' one of them said. 'Fancy having a
gorgeous-looking male like that actually staying in the
house!'

Vaguely startled, Elise queried, '*Is* he?' She hadn't

thought about whether he was good-looking. She supposed, in a rugged, careless way he could be called hand-
some.

Another girl laughed. 'She's only got eyes for Peter,
silly! She's just engaged, remember.'

Elise smiled at the general laughter, surprised at the
strength of her reluctance to introduce Shard to these
girls. She supposed it was because they weren't of his
world—no, he wasn't of theirs. She knew he wouldn't
be interested in any of them. And suddenly she thought
it would be amusing to introduce him to these girls. They
had gone to the best schools, most of them to her own
school, they had been presented as debutantes with her,
they were well educated and came from well-off families,
were poised and pretty and accustomed to sophisticated
men.

'He's a labourer,' she said. 'An unemployed builder's
labourer. You know how Gary's always picking up
strays. Be nice to him. He's out of his depth and he has
no conversation.'

She introduced him to five girls, one by one, and
watched them being nice to him. He danced with them
all. He didn't look at her. She danced with Peter, and
sometimes with others, and watched Shard with his arms
about other girls, the lazy grin that he slanted at them
from time to time lightening the near-boredom on his
face. She waited for him to seek her out, but he didn't.
She thought he should have the manners to ask Gary's
sister for one dance. And he didn't.

Once she saw him standing alone, leaning on a pillar.
She went over to him with a bright, hostess smile and
said, 'Are you enjoying yourself, Shard?'

'Yes,' he said. 'Thank you.'

'You're not dancing.'

'I've been dancing, a lot.'

'There are some very nice girls here.'

'I know. You introduced me to some of them.'

Suddenly shakingly angry, she controlled her voice and smiled straight into his eyes, her eyes limpid. 'I asked them to be nice to you,' she said. 'Specially.'

She saw at once that he had guessed exactly how, and she could have borne it better if he had been angry. But the answering smile he turned on her held nothing but pure enjoyment, his voice broken only by the threat of laughter. 'How kind of you, Elise,' he said. 'You're very like your mother.'

She turned and walked away, unable to face him any longer. It would have been kinder if he had hit her. She almost wished that he had; she could have hit him back, then. Her hands itched to do it. She wanted to fight him, to watch him flinch as she struck out at him and felt the sting of his hard flesh against her hand.

CHAPTER THREE

THERE was nothing Elise could do but go on with the party, making sure everyone was enjoying themselves, keeping the music and the food going.

After eleven a cold breeze sprang up, and the crowd moved inside. They spilled through all the rooms and some of the older ones left before midnight. The noise swelled near twelve o'clock, then hushed expectantly as Howard called for silence before the hour.

Elise stood with Peter, his hand loosely on her waist, and they kissed as the clock struck the hour. Everyone was laughing around them and there was the usual singing of Auld Lang Syne and a lot of kissing. When she felt hands pluck her away from Peter's side, she turned with a smile, not knowing at first who it was.

She saw grey eyes blazing in a dark face, and gasped. And then hard hands clasped her waist, pulling her against him, and a hard mouth touched hers, pressing her head back, bruising her lips against her teeth. She tasted blood before he released her, and she fell back against Peter's steadying arm as Shard turned away.

She heard Peter mutter, 'He's got a nerve, hasn't he?'

'Oh, don't be so stuffy, Peter!' she snapped, immediately appalled and contrite. She smiled to soften the words. 'It was nothing,' she said. 'Scarcely a kiss at all. Everybody does it at New Year.'

It had lasted only a few seconds, and she didn't know if it could come under the general heading of a kiss. She felt—branded.

*

They spent New Year's Day at the beach, picnicking on cold ham and chicken, strawberries and champagne, and spending a lot of time in the water. Gary brought a surfboard and it turned out that Shard was very good at surfing. He looked magnificent standing on the board riding in on a high breaker, and Elise couldn't bear to watch him. She went for a long walk with Peter along the sand and over the rocky headland at the end of the beach. Tiny black mussels clung to the rock and cut her feet, and blue crabs scuttled into cracks ahead of them with a scratching sound, and as the tide flung itself against the rocks in increasing swells, washing into the pool and disturbing the tiny starfish and shrimps, hermit crabs and seaweed crabs that peopled them, Peter began to worry about getting back.

They had to scramble through thigh-deep water in the sand to reach the soft sand again, Peter frowningly anxious, and Elise laughing and nonchalant, as the waves pushed and sucked at them, the spray in their faces.

Gary and Shard were lying on towels near the big beach umbrella where Katherine sat, elegant in a boutique sundress and big sunglasses, on a mohair rug, and read a new bestseller that her husband had given her for Christmas.

Elise and Peter shared a large beach towel, putting suntan lotion on each other's backs, lying close together, her head pillowed on his shoulder, and one knee raised. Shard hadn't moved since they came back, but she knew that he was watching her. He watched her all the time.

They packed up early because more people were expected for drinks that evening. Elise, who was tired of parties, wished that her mother didn't see the Christmas–New Year season as an endless round of hospitality. She tended to use the week to gather in one fell swoop all the people she might have missed issuing invitations to through the year, or those she hoped would issue her and Howard some in the new year.

Peter was spending the evening with his own parents, and Elise was rather relieved. He hadn't left her side all day, and she had noticed towards the end of the afternoon his frequent annoyed glances at Shard. She didn't look at Shard herself. She concentrated all her attention on Peter, knowing that Shard was watching, knowing that she wanted him to watch her, and hoping he didn't want to, that he couldn't help himself.

She put on a slim, cool, dark blue patio dress with a deep neckline and halter tie at the neck, and no jewellery. The people invited tonight were business acquaintances of her father's, and they wouldn't stay late.

She was handing around dainty canapés to the guests as they sat in a rough semi-circle in the lounge, when someone turned to Shard, at ease with a drink in his hand, his long legs stretched from the depths of a leather chair. 'Shard——' the woman said interestedly. 'What an unusual name.'

'My birth certificate says Sherard,' he told her. 'My mother liked upper-crust names. But somehow it got shortened to Shard, and it stuck.'

Howard's voice struck in with, 'What do you mean, *upper-crust*, Shard? We don't have any class distinction in New Zealand. You know that.'

Shard didn't look around the room at the real leather of the armchairs, the thick pile of expensive carpet, the original paintings on the wall, or remind them of Katherine's casual mention of her family, land-owners since the pioneering days, connected to English nobility. He looked at his host and after the briefest of pauses said, 'Yes. Of course.'

Katherine, sitting beside her husband, smiled at Shard and asked lightly, 'Well, what *did* you mean, then,

Shard?' as though she could have no idea and awaited enlightenment.

Gary said, 'It was just a figure of speech, Mother.'

Shard glanced at him and said, 'Sure,' and raised his drink to his lips.

But Katherine was not to be deflected. 'Your mother's dead, and your father too, I believe, Shard? Gary said you had no people.' She turned to the other guests and added, 'That's why Gary brought Shard to spend Christmas with us. So sad, to have no family at this time, isn't it?'

Having effectively focused their attention on him, she returned to the attack. 'By the way, Shard, what did your father do?' She took a canapé from the plate that Elise held, standing beside her, and added, 'For a living, I mean?'

Elise's fingers tightened on the plate, and she turned to look at Shard, forgetting to hand the savouries on to the man seated at the other side of her mother. Echoes of her childhood returned suddenly and she felt her breath stop in her throat. *No*, she thought, *don't do this, Mother*!

Shard looked unperturbed, his half-empty glass steady in a negligent hand, his shoulders relaxed against the wide back of the chair. Without hesitation he said easily, 'I believe he got quite good at making mailbags, Mrs Ashley, but I don't know if you'd call it a living. He spent most of my childhood in prison.'

There was an electric silence, while the guests tried to look as though they hadn't heard, and two flags of colour appeared in Katherine's cheeks.

Gary said, his voice strained, 'I thought you were an orphan, Shard.'

Shard turned to look at him, apparently unaware that he had said anything untoward. 'Virtually. My mother died when I was five or so and I was brought up in institutions. Most kids in orphanages these days aren't true orphans, you know. Those get adopted. Children's homes cater for those whose parents are living but can't —or don't want to—care for them.'

One of the women said quickly, 'Yes, I've *heard* that! It reflects the state of our society, don't you think? All the broken homes these days——'

General conversation broke out and Elise went on passing the plate of savouries around the circle.

She kept her eyes on the plate she was holding as she reached Shard. She said quietly, 'I'm going for a drive later. Would you like to come?'

The slight pause before he answered might have indicated surprise. Then he said, 'Yes. When?'

'I'll let you know,' she said, and passed on.

He sat beside her in silence as she drove along the southern motorway into the gathering dusk. Lights were flickering on in the houses alongside as they passed the outer suburbs of the city, and a deep purple haze hung over the farther hills as they moved into rolling green countryside. Elise turned off on to a side road and switched on the headlights, picking up grasses waving in the evening breeze by the roadside, and passing shadowing macrocarpas. She changed gear, swept round a corner and put down her foot on the accelerator. The car leaped forward and flew down a long straight, over a broad, shallow hill, into a dip and over a steeper, longer rise. A rabbit fled in panic at the side of the road, and an early oppossum loped away from the beam of the lights, amber eyes gleaming huge.

'What did your father do?' she asked, her eyes on the road. 'To get sent to prison.'

'Which time?'

She looked at him then, briefly, to see if he was being
sarcastic.

He wasn't. 'He was what's called a habitual criminal,'
he told her. 'Petty thefts, burglary, receiving. Not a
grand, romantic crime of passion—not murder or a
clever bank robbery. Just sordid, cheap little criminal
activities. Disappointing, isn't it?'

She couldn't mistake the mockery in that. She braked,
suddenly, so that Shard had to brace himself with a hand
on the dashboard, and the car slid to a stop at the brow
of a hill, the lights of the city winking at them from the
distance on the dark harbour's edge.

Not looking at him, Elise asked levelly, 'What do you
mean by that?'

'This sudden interest in me. I know your style, Elise.
The moneyed background, the best school, the sheltered
life style and eventually the right marriage with a guy
from the same sort of family as your own. Only every so
often you feel the need to break out and show your
independence, live a little dangerously, take a fashionable swipe at your parents' values. Your small rebellions
never last long, they just liven up your life a bit, and
you'll soon settle down and become a replica of your
mother—a little younger, a little more liberal, but a
reasonably faithful carbon copy. I thought, when I first
saw you, that you were something different—unique.
But you're cut from the same basic pattern as all the
other spoilt little rich girls you know. What did you
hope for from a drive in the dark with the son of a
criminal? Just a few hours of worry for your parents, to
show them you're all grown up and able to take care of
yourself? Or something a bit more exciting? Are you
hoping I'll make a pass at you? Try to rape you, perhaps?'

'Have you finished?' she asked between her teeth. She

still hadn't looked at him. Her hands gripped the wheel in front of her. She turned her head at last and in the darkness her eyes blazed up at him. 'Now *you* can listen for a change. I'm not remotely *interested* in you, Shard Cortland, so don't flatter yourself! I asked you to come with me because I was *sorry* for you, that's all—as I'd be sorry for a dog that got accidentally kicked. You're not a person to me, you're one of Gary's stray dogs—he was always bringing home misfits and oddities as a child, it's a habit he's never grown out of. And it always annoyed my mother. Sometimes she can't help showing it. It was stupid of me to think you might have been hurt, tonight. You deliberately caused a sensation because you have an outsize chip on your shoulder about people who happen to have been luckier than you. You enjoyed shocking my mother's guests—I wouldn't be surprised if you made up that story about your father just to draw attention to yourself.'

'Wrong.'

She shrugged. 'All right. But you chose to admit to it because you wanted to embarrass my mother.'

'I chose to admit it because I was asked and because it was the truth.' Shard spoke flatly, not as though he was defending himself, but as though it didn't matter, because he didn't give a damn what anyone thought. He was impervious to her mother's hints, to her own insults. She wasn't as tough as he. His assessment of her character had stung.

'Why did you come to stay?' she asked him. It hadn't been because he had nowhere to lay his head, she was sure, or because he missed having a family round him at Christmas time. 'Did you want to see how the other half lived? I hope we lived up to your expectations—*I*, at least, seem to have confirmed your prejudices about rich girls.'

He said, 'I came because Gary asked me to, and I like him.'

'I'm sure he's flattered. You don't like the rest of us, do you?'

'Does it matter?' he asked, betraying a hint of curiosity, as though he couldn't quite understand that anyone should care whether other people liked them or not.

'Not to me,' she said. 'Actually, I can hardly wait until you go.'

'Then it matters.'

'Not at all.' She stopped on the next breath, a long training in good manners intervening.

As though he knew, Shard said, 'Go on.'

'No.' She wanted to tell him she disliked him, more than anyone she had ever met before. But he was waiting for her to say it, and she wouldn't let him make her do it.

She started the car and turned it in a tight, fast circle, the tyres throwing up loose metal in their wake, and headed for the winding, narrow road that led to the top of that special hill.

She threw the car around the curves recklessly, the headlights plunging ahead of them, the wheel swinging in her hands as she negotiated the blind corners, using instinct and memory as much as sight. She had never driven this way at night before, never driven over this road quite as fast as this.

She looked at Shard once, and saw that he had braced himself in the corner, one arm along the back of the seat, the other lying along the door. The breeze ruffled his hair and his teeth showed white in silent laughter.

She stopped at the top so suddenly that the back of the car swung off the road a little before it came to a halt.

Elise sat with her head thrown back for a moment, savouring the quiet, the sharp, dampish smell of the bush at night, taking a long breath of cool, clean air.

She opened her door and got out to walk to a gap in the trees where the hillside sloped steeply away and the lights of the city could be just glimpsed between a fold in the hills, making a faint glow in the sky that merged with the stars. A high moon scudded overhead and silvered the leaves on the dark trees nearby. There were crickets singing and somewhere far into the bush a more-pork called sadly.

Elise heard Shard leave the car and come over the stones of the road. She felt him at her back before he reached her, and whirled about, suddenly finding it unbearable to wait with her back to him.

He stopped three feet from her, and said, 'I wasn't going to touch you.'

'You startled me,' she said.

He didn't answer or apologise, and she thought it was because he knew that it wasn't true.

She said, 'We'll go back.' And he shrugged and stood aside for her to pass him.

As she did so he didn't move, but her skin reacted as though he had reached out and caressed her, a shivering warmth creeping along her bare arms, and as she slid behind the wheel she realised that the hollow sinking in her stomach was disappointment, that the tension that had gripped her was sliding into depression. And she knew with humiliation that it was because she had wanted him to touch her. To put his arms about her and hold her, kiss her . . .

He got in and as he leaned back to close the door, his shoulder and arm brushed her and she started violently, moving away from him.

He turned slowly to look at her. Elise put out a shaking hand to switch on the ignition, and he caught it in strong fingers, pulling her round by her wrist to face him.

'*Don't!*' she exclaimed. 'Leave me alone!'

'But you don't really want me to,' he said, and pulled her into his arms.

She fought him silently, trying to push against his unyielding chest, flinging her head back to evade his mouth. But her hands were imprisoned between them, and long, hard fingers held her head still while he found her mouth with a kiss that was like a blow.

She was conscious of his hand flat against the smooth skin of her back, bared by the halter-necked dress she still wore. His thigh pressed against hers, and his mouth was merciless, pressing her head against the upholstery of the seat back, then his hand shifted to caress her neck, the thumb gently sliding over the little hollow below her ear.

She managed a little protesting jerk of her head and Shard lifted his lips a fraction from hers and muttered, 'Kiss me back, Elise.'

'Like *hell*——'

He moved swiftly and captured her lips again, parted on the words. His mouth prised them further apart and began a more gentle, tantalising exploration, and a slow fire seemed to trickle over her skin. She gave a little whimper of stunned protest, knowing her mouth was softening for him, her body losing its resisting stiffness.

Against her mouth, he murmured, 'No, like heaven ...' And she felt his hand on her breast as though it was his right to cup and mould it in his palm and enjoy its softness as his mouth enjoyed the softness of hers.

She had stopped struggling altogether, her palms flat against his chest, feeling the pounding of his heart against her fingers, her head still tipped back while Shard dragged his mouth down her throat and kissed her shoulders and lower, where the deep neckline exposed the beginning curves of her young breasts.

His hand moved against her back, and she took a deep breath of pleasure, but when she felt his fingers on the knot at her nape that held the halter top in place, she suddenly recoiled away from him, shocked back to sanity.

She had thrown herself back against the door like an animal at bay, but he didn't try to follow her. He sat still where she had left him and commented, 'You're very true to type.'

'You surely didn't expect me to let you——'

'No. I didn't expect it.'

His tone said he had known just what to expect from her, the tactics of a spoiled, rich little virgin, out for thrills. And she wanted to hit him for it. But that would be running true to type, too, she supposed. She wouldn't give him the satisfaction.

She fumbled in the little shelf by the steering wheel for cigarettes and lit one, took a deep draw and expelled the smoke carefully through pursed lips. 'You don't smoke, do you?' she asked him, in a cold, polite little voice.

'No.'

'You should try it.' She took another deep draw on the cigarette. 'With luck, it might kill you in time.'

His white smile in the darkness acknowledged the jibe. As the cigarette went to her mouth again, he said, 'You'll have to try harder than that.' And he bent swiftly, catching her wrist to hold it away from them while he kissed her, and she felt the smoke on her breath fill his mouth.

The effect was amazingly erotic, and she thought, *damn him, damn you, Shard Cortland*! She had just been regaining her equilibrium, and now she was shaking again.

She hoped the smoke would choke him, but when he

moved away from her again he was smiling.

She opened the ashtray and stubbed out the half-smoked cigarette viciously, snapped it shut and started the engine. She thought, *in two more days he'll be gone, and I hope I never see him again!*

She tried to forget him, after he had gone. It should have been easy. He left nothing behind, and her mother only once referred vaguely to that 'awkward young man Gary brought home for Christmas.'

'My father seemed impressed with him,' Howard said from behind his paper.

Katherine gave an edgy little laugh. 'Your father would like anyone who had the patience to listen to his interminable reminiscences.'

'Yes, maybe. I believe the young fellow visited him once or twice.'

'What? Why?'

Howard shrugged. 'He seemed to like the old man.'

'I think you should put a stop to it.'

'For heaven's sake, Kate——!'

'Really, Howard, for a businessman you're surprisingly naïve, sometimes. Don't you realise that young man is on the make? He wangled an invitation from Gary, who heaven knows has *nothing* in common with a boy of his type—he dropped blatant hints while he was here that you should offer him a job—he even embarrassed Peter by positively *rudely* staring at poor Elise, who fortunately is too sensible to be taken in by that kind of vulgar flattery——'

Elise looked up, flushing and startled. 'Mother, I——'

'I know, dear, you very wisely refused to encourage him, and Peter was quite right to ignore the whole business——'

'Kate!' Howard interposed. 'I think you're letting

your imagination run away with you. I don't recall any blatant hints, as you call them—as a matter of fact I thought of offering him a job, but Gary advised me not to.'

'There! You see, even Gary saw through him at last!'

'Nothing of the kind. He thought he would be too proud to accept.'

Katherine gave a hard laugh. 'He must have over-played his hand, there. Gary took him at his word, then, and serve him right. Oh, Howard, can't you see? A boy like that with a criminal background—you know, your father still has control of quite a lot of money, Howard, even since you took over the business and he retired ...'

'Yes, but——'

'Well, I've warned you.' Katherine swept out of the room with the air of having washed her hands of the affair, leaving Howard looking thoughtful and vexed, and Elise tense and dismayed.

'My dear,' her father said, 'your mother is sometimes very shrewd about people. I must say Shard didn't strike me as—though I did wonder why an intelligent young man of twenty-five hadn't settled in a regular job ... *Did* he stare at you, as your mother said?'

'I hardly looked at him,' said Elise. 'How would I know?'

Her father said frowningly, 'He did kiss you, though——'

Her head flew up, eyes wide with shock, even as her father added, 'At the New Year's Eve party——'

But he had seen her face, and as she stammered with relief, 'Oh, *that*!' his eyes sharpened, and he looked at her closely.

'That wasn't the only time, then,' he said. 'Elise?'

She jumped to her feet, her face hot. 'It was nothing, Dad.'

'You should have told me——'

'There was no need—it only happened once, and—and it simply wasn't important enough to bother about, anyway. I can cope with—boys.'

'Well, as your mother says, you've always been a levelheaded youngster, Elise. I suppose—I hadn't thought about it, but you could be a target for an unscrupulous, good-looking layabout. I'm glad you've got Peter. You'll be all right with him.'

Elise had started her second year at art school, glad to be busy once again with classes.

She left the building one hot day at the beginning of March and walked slowly to her car, because the tar was sticky and bubbling on the footpath and the slightest sign of haste was enough to bead her upper lip with tiny drops of perspiration. She kept her eyes on the ground in the car park, because she didn't want her light, high-heeled sandals covered with melted tar and wanted to avoid the soft spots on the heat-shimmering tarseal. The summer lingered late this year, the blistering heat must lift soon into autumn.

She lifted her eyes when she neared her car, and her feet stopped for a split second as she saw Shard leaning against it, in lean-fitting denims and a loose shirt open nearly to his waist.

Elise stepped closer and said, 'Hello, Shard. What are you doing here?' and smiled to cover a flutter of nervousness.

He didn't smile back. 'Waiting for you,' he said curtly.

'Should I be flattered?'

He didn't even bother to answer that. 'Shall we talk here or drive to somewhere cooler?' he asked.

She debated arguing the point about whether they had anything to talk about, but his manner told her he was unlikely to take no for an answer, and she certainly didn't feel up to arguing with him in this heat.

She shrugged and said, 'Let's drive.'

He got in beside her and she took them down Queen Street with its verandahed shops at the top and the tall multi-storey office buildings at the foot of the hill as it swept down to the harbour, then turned right on to Tamaki Drive and followed the route around the edge of the water past Mission Bay.

She drew up finally beneath an old pohutakawa that still held a few scarlet blossoms among the silver-backed leaves that laid a blessed umbrella of shade over them, and stopped with the bonnet of the car facing the sea.

Shard cast a cursory glance at the tanker making its stately way into the harbour, the ferry plying across to the North Shore, squat and busy as it ploughed a foaming wake across the green water, and the distant yachts dipping and careening below the high span of the harbour bridge.

Then he turned to look at her, his grey eyes light and hard. 'What exactly did you say to your father about me?' he asked.

Genuinely surprised, she frowned in puzzlement. 'Nothing. What are you talking about?'

'Your father has given instructions I'm not to be allowed to see your grandfather. At least he had the guts to tell me himself, but what I can't figure out is that one of the reasons seems to be that I'm supposed to have attacked you. So you kiss and tell—lies, do you?'

'*Attacked*——?' Horrified, Elise suddenly understood. Her father had been so certain that if Shard had kissed her, it must have been without her consent, that he had translated that into something much worse. 'Did he say that?'

'He implied it.'

'But—didn't you——'

'Deny it? My word against his darling daughter's?'

She looked away, biting her lip. 'I didn't go to him telling tales, Shard. I hardly said anything, just let slip something by mistake, and he jumped to conclusions. I'm sorry. I'll tell him that—that you didn't do anything I didn't ask for.'

'You admit that?'

With difficulty, she said, 'Yes.'

'You wanted me to kiss you, didn't you?'

Her cheeks hot, her eyes on the yachts in the harbour, she muttered between clenched teeth, 'Yes, yes, *yes*! I *wanted* you to kiss me!'

'Okay.' His hand closed over her clenched fingers, slipped to her wrist. 'Look at me.'

Elise pulled in a quick breath and turned to stare into his face. It looked grave and gaunt. His eyes were intent, with a silvery sheen. 'And I wanted to kiss you. I wanted nothing else from the moment I saw you. Or rather, I wanted that and a lot more. To kiss you, to touch you, to make love to you. I want you.'

Her lips parted in surprise and she touched her tongue to them. 'But . . .'

'Sure, I stayed away from you. Since New Year. I survived—I've never needed anyone, I don't need you. I'm not asking for your love—I've never had any use for love. Only I want you like hell.'

The blunt, brutal statement shocked her into movement. She jerked away the hand that he still held and said, 'Well, too bad. You can't have me!'

Shard just stayed looking at her, unsmiling and still. Then he said, the flatness of his voice making it a denial rather than a query, 'Can't I.'

Elise drew a painful breath and muttered, 'Get out of my car!'

He grinned and opened the door and climbed out, standing with his hands on his hips and watching as she manoeuvred the car back on to the road. The chrome of the bumper grazed his denim pants as she passed, but he didn't move.

She wanted never to see him again.

But she did. About a week later he was waiting as she left the door of the school, with a couple of brown paper bags in his hands, wearing new but dusty jeans and a neat denim shirt.

'Have lunch with me,' he invited. 'I've brought it,' lifting the bags, and Elise saw that they held sandwiches and sweet cakes and two cans of fruit juice.

They sat under a tree in the nearby park, with the other students and office workers who sprawled under the trees or sat on the green wooden seats or on the stone steps that broke the steep paths.

Looking at his clothes, she asked, 'You've got a job?'

'Yes.'

'What is it?'

His eyes gleaming with mockery, he said, 'It's a job.'

Elise picked up a crust off her sandwich and threw it to a pigeon that had alighted near them, gleaming eyes expectant. Let him be mysterious, then! She wasn't going to show any more interest.

Shard took the tab off one of the cans and handed her the drink. It was cool and sweet, and as she tipped her head to drink it she was aware of his eyes on the long line of her throat.

She cradled the can in her hands and looked back at him, her eyes acknowledging the desire in his, her smile deriding it.

He moved, leaning back against the tree, his head back,

lips parted in silent laughter, his grey eyes gleaming at her.

Caught unaware by a sudden spiralling of excitement, Elise looked away, making an effort to breathe normally.

Abruptly, she said, 'I spoke to my father.'

'I know.'

She looked at him quickly, and he said, 'The ban was lifted—probably because the old man made such a fuss when he heard about it. He thought your father was exceeding his rights—or duties.'

She felt a stirring of anger. It hadn't been easy for her, the interview with her father, and Shard seemed to be saying it hadn't even been necessary. He might at least have thanked her, she thought resentfully.

'I have to go,' she said, standing up.

He sat where he was, perfectly at ease. She said, 'Thanks for the lunch.'

Shard shrugged, watching her face with lazy interest. She thought he looked younger today. She had been surprised when her father mentioned his age; she would have thought he was older than twenty-five. 'Goodbye,' she said pointedly, and he grinned and said casually, 'So long, Elise.'

But he came again, and although Elise had promised herself to have nothing further to do with him, she went along with his casual invitations, salving her conscience by telling herself there was nothing in it but an odd kind of friendship. They never touched, they didn't talk of the pull of attraction that kept them seeing each other, the thing that she knew Shard despised in himself as much as she did in herself.

They talked. Sitting in her car watching some quiet corner of the harbour, or further afield in the high, bushcovered Waitakeres overlooking the city, strolling on the warm sand of quiet beaches, or climbing leaf-strewn paths through the damp silence of the bush.

Shard told her briefly about his childhood in 'homes' for children who had no home, and at more length about the jobs he had worked at since he left school, working on roads, on construction sites, for a time on board a cargo ship, for a year or so in a mining town in Australia. Construction was best, he said. Building excited him.

By contrast her own life seemed uninteresting, but he made her tell him about her childhood, and when she said, 'Why are you looking like that? I told you it wasn't interesting,' he laughed at her and refused to answer.

'Are you good at art?' he asked her once.

'Not very. Not more than competent. I might be able to earn a living as an illustrator or in a commercial art studio. I like it and I didn't want to teach, or go to university.'

She tried to draw him, but couldn't get it right, in the end screwing up the page and throwing it away in disgust. Shard rescued it and straightened it out, looked at it and said, 'You're right.'

Elise laughed, and he looked up enquiringly as his strong fingers crushed the paper again and consigned it back to the wire litterbasket.

'You'll never get on in business,' she told him. 'You're too honest.'

Quietly he asked, 'Does business have to be dishonest?'

'No, of course not—really. Only you're so—uncompromising. Maybe it's a reaction.'

'From what?'

She hesitated. 'From your father's habitual dishonesty?'

His face closed, he said, 'Maybe.' And then, 'Come on, we'll get back.'

When she was with him Elise was totally convinced of

his integrity, but sometimes the conviction wavered when she was away from him. Nothing she actually knew of him. was reassuring, and she couldn't forget her mother's assertion that he was 'on the make', and her father's worried admission that her mother was a shrewd judge of character. She herself had no experience by which to judge him impartially.

He said one day as they fed the pigeons in the park with the remains of their sandwiches, 'Come out to dinner with me.'

'Tonight?'

'If you like.'

Peter was away, it would be nice to have dinner with Shard. Usually their time together was snatched and brief, an hour or so for lunch, or a brief drive before she hurried away to get home or meet Peter. When she said, 'I have to get back now,' to Shard, he never protested or asked why, and she never explained. She never mentioned him at home.

She said, 'All right. Where shall I meet you?'

'I'll call for you.'

'No!'

There was a brief, tense silence. Elise felt his anger, but he said nothing.

'I've got a car,' she said. 'I'll pick you up. It's silly for you to come all the way to fetch me.' She laughed shakily, 'Haven't you heard about the New Woman? We don't have to wait around for men any more—aren't you lucky?'

Shard didn't laugh. He told her where to meet him and then she left. But she knew that he was angry because she hadn't wanted him to call at her home. She hoped he was going to be over it by the time she picked him up for their dinner.

As soon as he got into the car, looking her over in her

full-skirted silky dress with an unsmiling assessment, she suspected that he hadn't got over it. And when he told her where they were going, she knew it for sure. She tried to receive the news without showing the sinking of her heart, but the sharp, narrow-eyed grin he gave her as she turned the car immediately and without comment told her that he knew, anyway.

She knew that his preference would have been for somewhere quiet and unusual where the food was good and not necessarily exorbitantly priced, and that he knew very well where to find such a place.

But he had chosen instead to take her to a very well-known, very expensive, very popular restaurant where she was known and was almost certain to meet someone or other that she knew. And he had done it to punish her.

She hoped savagely that he would feel out of place there, that he would make a fool of himself. But he didn't. He acted with perfect confidence and asked the wine-waiter for his recommendation with an easy savoir-faire that belied simple ignorance, and sipped it with appreciation when it came. He consulted Elise's preference with suave courtesy and made unimpeachably polite conversation that made her want to scream with frustration, as they dined.

Instead she set her teeth, answered with an exquisitely overdone courtesy of her own, and drank a little too much of the very good wine while trying to avoid the curious stares of at least two people who she knew would be telephoning her mother and Peter's first thing in the morning.

The dinner seemed interminable, the wait between courses overlong. There was a tiny dance floor and music, but Shard hadn't suggested they dance, and she hoped

when the coffee came he would suggest that they leave
when they had drunk it.

Instead he grasped her wrist, and said, 'Let's dance.'

Elise rose obediently but was stiff and unyielding in his
arms. He pulled her close, his fingers digging into her
skin, and she stumbled. For an instant as his arm tightened to steady her, she felt his hard thighs against hers,
and heard his quick intake of breath as desire stirred his
body.

Immediately she felt the heat of the answering desire
in herself, and she jerked away from him, alarmed. The
hard barrier of his arm at her back stopped her movement, not letting her put more than an inch or two between them. His voice low but filled with laughter, he
asked, 'What's the matter?'

She said, 'I need some more coffee. I've had too much
wine.'

It was true, but what she needed most was to get away
from his unbearable nearness and collect herself, put up a
barrier of normality between them.

Shard ordered more coffee for her and watched while
she drank it. Then they went out into the cool night air,
and when he opened the car door for her and she climbed
in behind the steering wheel, he said, 'Move over, I'll
drive,' and gave her a push along the seat, taking the key
from her hand.

She knew it was no use protesting, and after all she
had admitted to drinking more than she should. Resentfully she fastened her seat belt and turned her head away
from him.

He drove along the harbour to one of the beaches they
had visited several times. In the daytime there would
have been strolling couples and mothers with young
children building castles and dashing in and out of the
shallow waves on the shore. Now the white strip of sand

was deserted and the lights from the opposite shore dipped raggedly into the dark harbour.

Shard got out and came round and opened Elise's door, pulling her out with a firm hand on her wrist. Her high heels struck into the soft sand and hard hands steadied her. Then he bent and lifted her ankles one by one and slipped off the shoes, tossing them back into the car. Elise knew deep down that she was being uncharacteristically docile, that she should protest, show some opposition to his ruthless, high-handed actions. But for once in her life she felt helpless, swept along by the dark force of a fiercely controlled emotion that she knew was in him.

CHAPTER FOUR

THEN Shard straightened and turned to face her, and he suddenly seemed close and menacing. The lethargy that had held her broke, and she instinctively stepped back from him.

He followed, and when she turned in panic he grabbed at her left wrist, pulling her round so that a sudden pain wrenched at her shoulder and she cried out, a gasping little shriek.

His other hand came up and hauled her taut body against his, and like ice brought in contact with heat, Elise melted, her only protest a sobbing little moan as Shard kissed her parted lips with a suddenly unleashed passion that demanded a total surrender.

Her hand clutched at his jacket to steady herself, because his arm moulded her body so tightly to his that her feet lost their balance, and she swayed against him.

He still held her wrist in a vice-like grip, but the pain of it was forgotten in the other sensations that were washing over her in hot sensual waves. His mouth seemed to be trying to draw her soul from her body, to be swallowed up in his. She hadn't known that a kiss could be like this, a raging, pitiless affirmation of power, a confident assertion of rights, an invasion of senses she hadn't known she possessed. She knew she could not deny him, that all the weeks they had met and talked and laughed and never touched had been only a preparation for this wonderful, terrifying explosion of touch and feeling.

When at last his mouth lifted from hers, she was panting, and his breath was harsh in his throat. In a drugged whisper, she said, 'Shard——' His mouth touched the curve of her shoulder, and she lifted back her head to give him access to the smooth skin of her throat. He still held her closely and she could feel the warmth and seduction of his masculine hardness against her breasts, her stomach, her thighs. His mouth moved lower over her heated skin, and she trembled, aware of an urgent need to be even closer. She felt his arm tighten and his head lifted. He was holding her left hand against his chest, and he moved his feet, lifting her a little away. She thought he was going to lower her to the sand, and she drew in a quick little breath, of expectation and fear and excitement.

The glitter of her engagement ring in the moonlight must have caught his eye. He lifted her hand and she felt him tug at the ring, and instinctively she curled her fingers. 'What are you doing?'

'Taking it off.' His voice was hard, an edge to it that cut into her bemused state of submission.

'No,' she said, the sound little more than a whimper, but her fingers clenched tightly. She had forgotten for the moment that it was Peter's ring. Only it had become a symbol of something other than her engagement. She was suddenly frightened of the power Shard had over her, of the mindless capitulation he had reduced her to.

Harshly he said, 'I won't make love to you while you wear another man's ring.' She felt her fingernail break as he prised her fingers away from her palm and she cried out as he twisted her wrist. His nails dragged over her skin as he pulled off the ring and flung it into the darkness across the sand.

'No!' she screamed as it arced away into the darkness. 'Shard, it cost an awful lot——'

He threw back his head then and laughed, and she attacked him with her fists, her nails, her bare feet. He backed, fending her off, then catching her wrists, taking her with him down on to the softness of the cool sand while she still fought him until he was holding her down with his legs pinning hers and her arms against the sand with his hands imprisoning her wrists. Exhausted, she lay panting, abusing him in a choked, sobbing whisper. There was a dark trickle of blood on his cheek where she had scratched him, and he had lost two buttons off his shirt. His breathing was not quite even, either, but as Elise stopped her useless struggles and lay inert, he smiled tightly down at her while she called him names that would have shocked her mother.

He muttered, 'Shut up, darling,' and bent his head to kiss her.

Elise shut her teeth and tightly closed her lips against him. He lifted his head and said grimly, 'You had no right to be wearing his ring.'

'I had every right!' she blazed. 'I love Peter and I'm going to marry him!'

She flinched away from the sudden movement of his hand as it left her wrist, turning her face aside. Nothing happened, and she slowly moved her head again to look at him.

He said, 'Yes, I *should* hit you for that. You little liar! You want me.' His fingers slipped into her dress, finding the proof.

'It—it isn't love,' she gasped. Her hand grasped at his wrist, trying to drag his hand from her breast. '*Stop it!*'

He moved his hand upwards to her throat, spread his fingers against her collarbone. 'What's love?' he murmured, his lips against her earlobe. 'This?' His tongue slid along the little groove below her ear. 'This?' He moved and found her mouth with his, all the savagery of his previous kisses erased in a sweet, unbearable torment of desire. He raised his head and saw it reflected in the dark pools of her eyes, and with his hands on her again, he whispered, 'Does Peter make you feel like this, Elise?'

She didn't answer, her head going helplessly from side to side as he covered with his lips the swiftly beating pulse at the base of her throat.

Shard stopped her movement of denial with his mouth, and when he raised his head again, said, 'We belong together, you know it. You aren't going to marry Peter. You want me. Say it—tell me you want me, Elise.'

It was true, her body clamoured with the knowledge, but the word he used jarred. A faint coldness invaded the heat of her languorous desire, and from somewhere she summoned the willpower to say, on a hard gasp of protest, 'No!'

Shard kissed her again, his mouth searchingly possessive. 'Say yes!' She shook her head and tried to turn away, but his lips found her again.

She dragged her mouth away and cried out, 'No——! No, no, no!'

His hands were on her shoulders, the fingers tightening until they bit into the softness of her flesh. Harshly, he said, 'I could take you, anyway.'

Her own voice hard with the effort she made to stop it trembling, she said, 'It's called rape, Shard.'

She heard the anger, the frustration in his indrawn breath, and then he suddenly rolled away from her, lying back on the sand, once knee raised and his forearm over his eyes.

Elise knew she had won. She lay where he had left her, wondering why she felt nothing but a kind of colourless despair.

With an effort she sat up, adjusting her dress where Shard had pulled it from her shoulders. Then she stood, feeling the gritty sand between her toes, surprised that her legs actually held her. She began to move down the beach and Shard got up and asked, 'Where are you going?'

'To look for my ring,' she said tiredly.

He said, 'Supposing you find it—what are you planning to do with it?'

'Put it back on.'

He caught at her arm. 'You can't marry him, Elise. You're going to marry me.'

The thought stopped her breath in her throat. 'I can't,' she protested. 'I can't do that!'

He shifted his grip to her shoulders. '*You can't marry Peter!*' he said fiercely.

Confused, panicky, she cried, 'Peter loves me—he needs me! He—he's solid and—and——'

'Safe? Is that what you want, after all? Safety and security and respectability? Is it so important to you?'

'It isn't that!' she cried, despairing of his understanding. 'And what can you offer me that's any better? What I feel for you is nothing but a basic animal instinct—you might be anyone with the right arrangement of genes. We have nothing in common but some sort of—of biological reaction!'

His hands leaving her, he said coldly, 'Is that what you think?'

'It's the truth,' she answered bleakly. 'I suppose I should be flattered that you offered me marriage,' she added, 'finally.'

Shard's head made a quick movement that she couldn't interpret.

'Finally?' he repeated. Then, his tone changing to a drawling note, he said, 'But of course, it's the classic gambit when a man can't get a girl any other way. Isn't that what you expected?'

'Expected?'

'Held out for. You've played a clever game, little rich

girl, and I'm letting you win. Now run along home before I change my mind.'

He took her car key from his pocket and she automatically took it. 'Shard——?' she queried, scarcely believing he really thought she had planned this, that she had been playing him along for fun.

'Shut up and go,' he snapped. 'Or dear Peter won't get the virgin bride he's expecting.'

She stepped back from him, then fled across the sand to the car.

Miraculously, she got her ring back. She drove to the police station nearest to the beach the next morning to report it lost, and it had already been handed in by an early morning swimmer, who had found it before it was irretrievably buried in the sand.

Elise left some money as a reward for the honest swimmer, and when the policeman said, 'Better put it on, hadn't you, Miss Ashley? Don't want to lose it again,' she smiled quickly and did as he suggested.

'Seems quite tight,' he said, gazing thoughtfully at the scratches on her ring finger, and his face assumed a consciously bland look. 'You're lucky to get it back. Better take more care in future.'

She had to endure her mother's puzzled concern when she learned who had been her daughter's escort that evening. Elise explained, 'I met him yesterday and he suggested dinner, and as Peter isn't here, I was at a loose end, and didn't see why not. He really looks quite respectable these days, Mother. He has a job, apparently.'

'I don't think that Peter would——'

'Peter doesn't own me, Mother,' Elise said sharply.

'Elise! You are engaged to him—I should think he's entitled to a certain loyalty.'

'It was only a dinner, Mother! I won't be seeing him again.'

Peter came back from his trip a day early and called round, surprising them. When Elise opened the door to him, he smiled and said, 'Missed me, darling? I couldn't wait to get back to you.'

She met his kiss with her arms about his neck, clinging. Pleased at her reaction, he prolonged the kiss, and when they broke apart, pulled her back into his arms, his own trembling a little as they closed about her. 'I love you so much!' he whispered in her ear. 'I hate having to wait so long.' Her arms tightened about him, and he groaned. 'I need you, Elise,' he muttered. 'This week has been hell——'

She let him kiss her again, and stroked his hair. His need, his tenderness, were like a balm on her bruised nerves, her sore heart.

'Why should we wait?' she said. 'I'll talk to Dad.' She knew her mother would have no objection to an earlier wedding. 'Yes,' she said, touching her lips to his again as he started to protest. 'I want to marry you soon, Peter, as soon as possible—please!'

Three weeks later, after a frantic rush of preparation which gave her, as she had wanted, no time to think, she walked down the aisle of a fashionable church, stifling a rising panic with the repeated axiom that it was just wedding nerves, and became Mrs Peter Westwood.

When they returned from their honeymoon, it was to learn that Shard Cortland had borrowed a large sum of money from old Mr Ashley and left the country for Australia.

'Borrowed!' Katherine Ashley said scornfully. 'That's the last he'll see of *that* money! Your father's getting senile, Howard—you'll have to get a power of attorney or something, before he's approached by some other con-man and taken for the rest of his money. I knew that young man was up to something no good—of course with his background, it was to be expected—can't the lawyers do something about getting the money back, Howard?'

· 'The papers were drawn up by lawyers,' Howard said wearily, obviously not for the first time. 'The loan is to be paid back in a lump sum, with the interest, in ten years' time. It's unusual but not illegal. I told you, nothing can be done, unless the loan is not repaid when it comes due.'

'In ten years? The old man will be dead by then!'

'You're looking pale, darling,' Peter told Elise as they drove to their new home. 'Are you tired?'

'Yes,' she said. *And sick, and depressed.* She should have been glad, or at least relieved, that she had been sensible enough to turn down Shard, and marry Peter. He had proved beyond doubt now that he was everything her mother had said, out for what he could get from their family. She told herself she hated him, that everything he had said to her had been lies, that he had said he wanted to marry her because of what he hoped to gain from it if she had accepted.

That night was the first time she refused Peter, pleading her tiredness. He was understanding and considerate, and long after he had gone to sleep Elise lay beside him in their brand new double bed with slow tears trickling down her cheeks and dampening the fresh new pillow-slip that had been one of their wedding presents.

The double bed was sold along with the rest of the furniture from the house, at auction. Even Katherine, who was not sentimental, was slightly shocked at the wholesale way in which her daughter expunged the mementoes of her marriage. She kept her wedding photographs, one or two presents given them by her own closest friends, Peter's watch which had been her gift to him, a pair of his cufflinks and some linen. Everything else went. She wore the watch and used the linen in her new furnished flat, a light, airy modern town house with its own private courtyard in a block of four overlooking the sea.

She had come back from her month in the Bay of Plenty looking thinner but tanned and clear-eyed. She said nothing about the long days walking along a deserted beach or sitting on the dunes sketching the wild water, the sea-birds and the rough windblown grasses that clung to the edges of the sand. Or the nights she lay awake listening to the pounding of the breakers on the beach. She had swum in the ocean, although the rip was strong and there were no life-saving teams, preferring the buffeting of the high-combed breakers to the quieter and safer estuary where family parties picnicked on the weekends.

She had climbed high white cliffs, pulling herself up by the roots of the ancient pohutukawas that dug their huge clawed roots into the rough clay and sandstone, and brushing aside the glossy leaves of the taupata to reach the top and throw herself down, panting, on the high edge, watching the inexorable flow of the sea flinging itself against the sand.

She thought about Peter calmly and with sadness, going over the years of their life together deliberately. She had to do that before she could put them aside and start another life alone.

And she thought about Shard, in spite of herself. When he came into her mind she would get up and do something active, climb, swim, run along the lonely sweep of the beach until she was exhausted, her breath coming in painful gasps, her legs aching with exertion. She didn't want to think about Shard, to remember what he had said to her.

Through a friend she was commissioned to illustrate a children's book about a little boy on holiday at the beach. She fixed up her small spare room as a modest studio, laid out some shells she had collected from her own holiday, and spent several hours each day recalling the curves of the beach, the bending of the bronze-coloured pingao grass against the sea breeze, and the tumbling heads of the spinifex hurtling along the sand before it. She faithfully drew the spiral convolutions and the intricate patterns of the shells she had, and in her drawings placed them carefully at the base of a rock, in the shadows of a clump of red-flowered flax, in the plump palm of the little boy's hand.

The little boy was no particular little boy that she knew, but she watched children in parks and playcentres and school playgrounds and sketched them, and then went home and drew the little boy, still with a remnant of baby fat, sturdy-legged and round-eyed, with straight brown hair falling in a ragged, fine fringe over his innocent forehead.

There were times when she knew very well she was drawing the child she might have had—she and Peter—the child they had lost before it was born. They had told her it would have been a boy.

But those moments of pain were rare. Elise found she could become absorbed in her work so that the hours flew by unnoticed, and the serenity that she craved above everything became easier to achieve.

She sometimes spent quiet evenings at her parents' home with a few friends, but she never entertained, herself. All other invitations were refused.

She had just eaten her solitary meal and washed up one evening when the doorbell rang, a long, imperative peal.

Her heart began pounding. She knew only one person who rang like that, who could stamp the imprint of his own forceful personality on anything as impersonal as a doorbell.

When she opened the door reluctantly, her mouth tight, Shard pushed it wide and walked in.

Elise said, her tone brittle, 'I don't recall inviting you in.'

'I don't recall asking permission,' he drawled, looking at her in the same way that she remembered, as though it was not only his right, but a right that she had given him. 'You look better,' he commented. 'Have you exorcised your ghost?'

Inwardly she quivered, as she turned to walk into the lounge. Shard followed, and she asked, stiffly motioning him to a chair as she sat down herself, 'How did you know where to find me?'

'I've always known where to find you.'

Elise sat very still, knowing he spoke the truth, that he had known about her hideout in the Bay of Plenty, that he could have followed her there, and hadn't.

She asked, her head lifting, 'Do you employ a detective agency?'

'Nothing so melodramatic.' His eyes laughed at her. 'I have friends in your family, you know.'

She hadn't known. She had thought he had dropped out of all their lives six years ago.

He told her, 'I still see Gary occasionally. And your grandfather.'

She didn't know why it was a shock, but it was. She curled her lips scornfully and said, 'Does poor Granddad still think he's going to get his money back from you?'

She saw the arrested look in his eyes, the faint drawing together of his straight brows, and knew she had hit a nerve, somehow.

Shard said slowly, 'He knows he'll get it back. With every cent of interest that's owing on it.'

Elise raised her eyebrows delicately, half-disbelieving. 'You've done quite well for yourself.'

'I have.' He stood up abruptly, half-turned from her, then swung back to look down at her face. 'What about you?' he asked. 'Are you all right for money?'

'Yes, of course.' She looked at him in surprise. 'Were you going to offer me money?'

'If you needed it.'

'In return for—what?' she asked.

His eyes met hers and for just an instant she saw the blankness of non-comprehension. Then he said quietly, 'You bitch, Elise.'

Colour flooded her cheeks, but she held his eyes. 'Why? It's a natural conclusion—you said yourself you're not kind, and that you—want me. You don't do anything for nothing, Shard, do you?'

'I do what I want.'

'*Not* with me!'

He looked at her and laughed, and she burst out, 'Oh, leave me alone, can't you!' She was standing up, facing him with anguished eyes.

'No.'

The flat monosyllable was a stone wall against which her angry protests fell unheeded. Gathering her forces again, she demanded, 'What is it you want from me? Are you hoping I'll break down again—cry on your shoulder? Do you still want to see me weep, Shard? Is that it? Well, hard luck—I'm not going to give you that pleasure again——'

'*My God!*' he exclaimed. 'Do you really think I enjoyed seeing you cry?'

'You said—you said that was what you wanted!' she
reminded him, her eyes accusing him.

'It was what you *needed*, you little fool!' he said
harshly. 'Don't you know that bottling all that emotion
up wasn't doing you any good? You had to let go sometime, and that was the right time for it to happen.'

Her eyes darkened with memory, recalling his goad-
ing, his taunting of her for her 'stiff upper lip' and the
way he had held her so closely while she wept against
him. But the humiliation of breaking down so thoroughly
in front of him still remained, still rankled.

Stiffly, she said, 'So you're an amateur psychologist,
too. How clever of you to know just what I needed, and
just when to make sure of it. Especially as I don't suppose you've ever shed a tear for anyone in your life!'

Shard's mouth hardened. 'You're determined not to
give an inch to me, aren't you? I thought by now you
might be ready to start living again——'

'I *am* living again,' she told him emphatically. 'And I
can do it without your help.'

'All right,' he shrugged, 'get on with it, then.' And he
turned to go to the door. Elise didn't follow, and he
turned in the doorway and looked at her again. His voice
was quiet, but it carried across the room. 'You're wrong,
you know,' he said. 'I have shed tears. The last time was
on the day that you married Peter Westwood.'

CHAPTER FIVE

ELISE visited her grandfather regularly. Being infirm, he didn't go about much except on special occasions, but he liked his family to visit him. The next time she called to see him, they chatted as usual, sitting on one of the shady verandahs that allowed the residents a pleasant view of shorn lawns and bright garden beds. But Elise was less attentive to his conversation than usual, and eventually he said a little sadly, 'I'm an old fool, Elise, boring you with my talk of the days when I was young and full of ambition and just starting out in business . . .'

'No, you're not!' she protested. 'I like listening to you —it's just that I—I have a lot on my mind just now.'

'Oh, yes, of course, my dear.' He patted her hand. 'I'm sorry.'

'It isn't that,' she said softly. 'Not exactly. Grandad——'

As she hesitated, he said encouragingly, 'Yes——?'

'Have you seen Shard Cortland lately?'

His old eyes sharpened. 'Why do you want to know that?'

She floundered, 'I just—I heard that he visits you sometimes.'

'Yes. What of it?'

'Nothing. Except—you gave him some money, didn't you——? Some years ago.'

'No. I *loaned* it to him, on a legally drawn up contract, as you father well knows. Did he put you up to this?'

'No, I just wondered—how do you know you can trust him? You scarcely knew him when you made the loan.'

'I knew enough. I know a winner when I see one. He'll pay me back, don't you worry. In fact—— Well, it's business, between Shard and me, girl. I can't talk about his affairs to you.'

So she learned nothing from that, and despised herself for trying to. What did it matter to her what Shard did? She hadn't seen him for weeks, and she could only suppose that he had meant it when he told her to get on with living her life as she had boasted that she could—without his help. She was angry with herself, because Shard had taken her at her word—and because it hurt.

She realised afterwards that he had left her alone for exactly a month after his disastrous visit to her flat. She had been to the supermarket three blocks away one day, walking to save petrol, and came home to find him waiting for her, leaning against the door with his arms folded.

Elise stifled a surge of relief, a rising gladness that he had not, after all, finished with her, telling herself that she wanted nothing to do with this man, that he was an opportunist and not to be trusted. But when he straightened and she saw the quick welcome in his eyes, she could only say weakly, 'Shard——'

He took the bag of groceries from her while she found her key, and walked into the kitchen as though he owned it, placing the bag on the tiled counter.

Then he turned to look at her critically. 'You're not looking as well as last time,' he observed.

'I've lost some of my tan,' she answered defensively.

'And some more weight,' he said. 'Have you been eating properly?'

'Yes, of course,' she said shortly.

But he was emptying the bag, subjecting the contents to a thorough and not exactly enthusiastic inventory. 'Sardines,' he said, taking out the tiny tin. 'Dried soup, fish fingers, TV dinners—good God, girl, didn't they teach you to cook at that fancy school of yours?' He turned to the refrigerator and opened that, finding the half-dozen eggs, the packets of sausages, the packaged meals in the freezer compartment.

'Shard!' she protested indignantly. 'You don't have any right——'

'We're going out,' he said. 'For dinner. Do you want to change?'

'Shard, I'm not! I'm not going anywhere with you! What makes you think you have the right to barge into my home, investigate my kitchen, and order me about? You're the most egotistical, arrogant bully I've ever met, and I'd have to be *mad* to go out with you! Don't you ever *ask*——?'

She saw the sudden light in his eyes, and caught her breath. 'Hardly ever,' he drawled, and moved suddenly, somehow trapping her with his hands against the bench on either side of her waist. 'So regard the exception. Will you have dinner with me, Elise?'

She looked away from him, her eyes on her clenched hands in front of her. 'I haven't been out since——'

'So? There has to be a first time.' Miraculously, his voice was low and almost coaxing. 'It's three months, Elise. Long enough to lock yourself away from life. And long enough, God knows, for me to be patient.'

Her eyes flew up then to his face, noting the grim twist to his mouth.

She whispered, 'Shard—*please*——'

She saw him controlling his impatience, his teeth snapping together. 'Okay, honey, leave it, then. Dinner —and that's all, for now. Right?'

She nodded, grateful for the unexpected touch of gentleness. Shard moved away from her and said, 'Do you want to put on something pretty?'

'Where are we going?'

'Do you have a preference?'

She shook her head, knowing that he wouldn't, at any rate, take her back to the scene of their last disastrous dinner together so long ago. 'I'll leave it to you,' she said, and felt suddenly lighthearted as he laughed.

She knew he laughed because for once she was being amenable, and she didn't mind. His laughter made her feel happy, and happiness was an emotion she seemed to have been a long time a stranger to.

Afterwards she was amazed at how much she had enjoyed herself that evening. She rationalised that it was the first time she had accepted an invitation of any sort since Peter's death, and that she had almost forgotten what it was to enjoy an evening out. And Shard had been, for him, unusually considerate and gentle. They went to a small, quiet restaurant that specialised in Eastern foods, and he made suggestions and watched her eat with an implacable interest that ensured she did justice to each dish.

They talked little. Elise mentioned the beach where she had been staying, and he said he knew it, and they discussed local landmarks. She said, 'I heard you were in Australia.' And he answered, 'Yes, for a while.'

She looked up questioningly, wondering why he had sounded reticent, and asked, 'How was it?'

'All right,' he said, and began speaking of the scenery and the people in a general way that she found interesting in spite of herself. Because she hadn't really meant, *How was the country?* but, *How did you get on? What did you do there?*

When he paused she said, 'I thought you lived in Wellington now.'

'I moved to Auckland,' he said. 'A couple of months ago.'

He was looking at her deliberately, but she refused to meet his eyes. She said hastily, 'I gather you've a desk job these days? No more labouring?'

He said, 'Yes, I've come up in the world a little—I don't work with my hands any more.' His voice was sardonic.

She looked up quickly. 'Shard, I didn't mean to sound —patronising.'

His cool eyes took in the distress in hers, and his hand briefly covered her fingers, the contact warm and disturbing. 'Eat up', he said quietly, dispelling the brief moment of tension between them.

Elise had the feeling in the next few weeks, during which she saw Shard often, that he put some effort into preventing tension. That made it quite different from the atmosphere of their previous acquaintance, when every moment they were together had been vibrant with it.

They had quiet meals together and leisurely days at the beach or wandering along cool paths in the bush, and when they spoke it was of general topics, scarcely touching on the personal. Occasionally Elise noticed a touch of impatience in the way Shard rose suddenly from a prone position beside her on sun-warmed sand to fling himself into the surf, or in the tightening of his jaw as he saw her into her flat and gave her a curt goodnight. And in the back of her mind she knew that his unnatural restraint couldn't last. But while it did she was content to let things ride and be carried along on a tide that seemed to promise a haven of protection, although she was not quite sure why she felt the need of it. She only knew that while Shard continued to surround her with undemanding and strangely comforting care, she was content. He made sure she ate properly, buying in groceries occasionally himself, and brushing aside her thanks and her protests, laughing at her attempts to pay him. When he took her out he made sure she was home in time to get a good night's rest, and sometimes would phone her in the evening, demanding to know what she was doing.

She never thought of lying to him. If she was working she would say so, and Shard would say, 'Go to bed.'

Sometimes she protested, but her concentration was broken anyway, and after crossly telling him to mind his own business and she would go to bed when it suited her, she would put the phone down on his laughter and, an exasperated smile on her own lips, do as he said.

She never told her parents that she was seeing Shard, but of course they were seen together and someone relayed the news to Katherine.

'I didn't know you were friendly with Shard Cortland,' she commented to Elise austerely next time she saw her daughter.

'He's been kind to me,' Elise told her defensively.

Katherine's eyebrows rose delicately, in evident disbelief. 'I expect he has a motive,' she said. 'Don't let him take advantage of your situation, dear, will you?'

Stirred faintly to annoyance, Elise asked, 'In what way?'

'Well, some men seem to think a young widow—or divorcee—is fair game. You *are* in a vulnerable position, you know. It's barely four months since Peter died, and you don't want to lay yourself open to gossip.'

'Have your friends been gossiping?'

'Elise! Of course not. One or two mentioned that you've been seen about with Shard, that's all. They were concerned about you.'

'I'm sure,' Elise said resignedly. 'I suppose it's no use

telling them we're friends, and nothing more.'

Katherine looked faintly sardonic. 'Just good friends, as the saying goes? My dear, don't be naïve!'

Elise smiled wryly. 'No, I'm sure that's the quickest way to convince them there's no smoke without fire. But in fact it's quite true.'

'Yes, well—if you take my advice you'll keep it that way. It's far too soon to be thinking of involving yourself with another man—yet, anyway.'

Quietly Elise said, 'I'm aware of that, Mother. I have no intention of getting involved with anyone.'

But the next time she went out with Shard, instead of seeing her to her door and bidding her a quick goodnight, he gently pushed her inside with a hand at her waist, and turned her to face him in the darkness, his fingers moulding the bones of her shoulders.

Her head lifted involuntarily and before she could protest, his mouth closed over hers.

Elise went rigid, and after a few moments Shard lifted his head, his hands sliding down her arms and back again to her shoulders, almost as though her lack of response had nonplussed him.

He didn't attempt to kiss her again, but when she tried to move away his fingers tightened and held her.

In a brittle voice she said, 'I don't want that, Shard. I'm sorry.'

'Are you?' he questioned grimly. 'I wonder.'

'What do you mean?'

He shrugged and let her go. 'Perhaps fighting me has become a habit with you.'

'That's not true! I don't want to fight you. I don't want to make love to you, either. Can't we be friends?'

'I want more than that, Elise.'

'Shard, it's too soon!'

'I'm not going to wait the regulation twelve months, Elise.'

Her head went up. 'You take a lot for granted!'

'What do you want, a proposal on my knees?' he asked roughly.

'Perhaps I don't want to get married again!' she cried. 'Had you thought of that?'

Jeeringly he said, 'Why, did life with Peter put you off the married state?'

Her hand swung back and flew up to connect with his lean, hard cheek, and she felt the sharp sting against her palm.

In the ensuing silence she sensed the iron control that he was exerting over his anger. Instinctively she stepped back, clenching her fingers over the stinging of her palm.

Then Shard swung on his heel and left without a word, closing the door behind him with a decisive snap.

She missed him when she didn't hear from him over the next few days, and wondered if he expected her to contact him and apologise. He had given her a telephone number, but she had never used it.

She had tea with her parents, and a man she had known for years and whose divorce had just become final asked her to take pity on him and join him for a film and supper the following evening. Simply to show herself that she had no need to stay home thinking of Shard, she accepted, and when Shard rang her the following day she coolly told him she couldn't accept his invitation because she had another date. She could detect no sign of disappointment in his voice as he asked, 'What about Saturday?'

'My parents are having a party,' she told him. 'I've told them I'll come.'

This time there was the slightest pause. Then he said, 'Okay, have a good time.'

The evening with the old friend was rather flat. Elise spent most of their hour over supper listening to the story of his divorce and the events leading up to it, and the film had been a forgettable one.

For her parents' party she dressed carefully but without enthusiasm, dabbed perfume on as a finishing touch, and even arranged her hair in a new style to do credit to her people. The guests would be mainly business acquaintances, she gathered, and she knew that for these affairs her mother always took great pains to make a good impression. She expected the party would be a fairly small and quiet affair, not really gay. Her mother felt that she could now with decorum be expected to attend such gatherings, provided nobody rushed things.

What she had not expected was to find Shard there.

Her mother, doing introductions said, smilingly, 'And of course you know Shard, darling——' And Elise thought that beneath the casual manner she watched them with sharp interest.

Shard nodded, unsmiling, but there was a hint of mockery in the cold grey of his eyes. Elise smiled politely at him and murmured, 'Of course.' She hoped her face looked equally cool and polite, and tried to keep it that way.

She moved on to speak to someone else, seething inside with anger at her mother, knowing there was nothing she could say. To make an issue of the lack of warning would only confirm whatever suspicions Kate already had that theirs was no casual friendship, and she had a deep instinctive need to keep their relationship, such as it was, with Shard, private. Especially she wanted to keep it guarded from her mother's deadly interest.

But she did say casually, later, while she helped her

mother pour coffee, 'I thought you disliked Shard.'

'My dear, in the interests of your father's business, I'm compelled to entertain a number of people I dislike.'

'But Shard isn't one of Father's contacts——'

'On the contrary, he seems to be quite an important one, these days. Cortland Construction is a very big firm, after all.'

'*What?* You mean *Shard* is—he's *that* Cortland?'

'But surely you knew? I thought you two were quite friendly?'

'No, I had no idea. I suppose I should have. I knew that there was an Australian connection, and the firm was expanding in New Zealand, but I thought it was an old-established company over the Tasman. I never dreamed of connecting it with Shard. Why, how could he have built it up in only a few years? They're getting enormous contracts!'

Tartly Katherine said, 'With your grandfather's money. Oh, I admit he seems to have paid half of it back, and the rest will follow, I daresay, as your father keeps telling me. And apparently he saved a remarkable amount himself by working, as your father says, like a dog for ten years and putting every penny he could spare into investment accounts. He bought himself into a partnership in Australia and then bought out the other partner, talked himself into some lucrative contracts, and then opened a branch here in New Zealand. Now he has one in Wellington and has just begun in Auckland. Your father, in fact, is positively dazzled by the man. He says he showed a singleminded drive for success, and Howard admires that quite ridiculously.'

'Then he didn't cheat Granddad out of his money,' Elise said slowly, and with caution; a weight seemed to be slowly lifting from her heart.

'Well, I still think the old man was extremely foolish

to trust him,' Katherine said grudgingly. 'Though it's turned out for the best. Of course, your grandfather likes to congratulate himself that he still retains his old business acumen. Personally, I think that luck came into it a great deal.'

Perhaps it had, to some extent, Elise thought, but Shard's determination had been the main factor, she had no doubt.

Her mother was saying, 'Surely he told you?'

'Perhaps he thought I knew,' said Elise. 'We haven't talked much about business matters.'

Her mother looked up sharply. 'Have you been seeing very much of him?'

Carefully Elise said, 'Not lately.'

'That's as well. After all, you're quite recently widowed, and as I warned you before, you should be careful not to encourage any speculation. Perhaps in a few months—then it might be acceptable.'

Surprised, Elise looked up from putting spoons out on the saucers. '*What* might be acceptable?' she asked.

'Well, taking an interest in a man,' her mother explained. 'Of course, it's much too soon to be thinking of such things yet. But Shard made it blatantly obvious that he was attracted to you that Christmas that he stayed with us. Of course, he's older now and less inclined to such infatuations, I suppose, but he has been taking some interest in you, I gather?'

Elise did not reply, and her mother went on, 'After all, one couldn't accuse him *now* of being after your father's money, he has plenty of his own. I know Peter left you well provided for, as one would expect, but with inflation being what it is these days, a good second marriage—eventually—might be the wisest thing for you.'

'To *Shard*?' Elise queried unbelievingly.

Her mother looked up from briskly stirring a bowl of cream and said, 'I can't say I've ever liked him, but I must be fair. It seems I have misjudged him in some directions, and now he's—— After all, money does smooth the rough edges, and there'll be plenty of other girls who realise that Shard Cortland is quite a catch, these days. He isn't a rather uncouth boy with no prospects *now*.'

Elise looked stunned. Never had her mother spoken so frankly to her before.

Colouring a little, Katherine went on defensively, 'It may seem a little insensitive to you, speaking of this so soon after Peter's death, my dear, but I'm your mother, and looking to your future welfare. I don't imagine I shall ever be fond of Shard as I was of dear Peter, but you're not a young girl any more—though certainly young enough to marry again, and marry well. It would be foolish, of course, to expect the romance of a first marriage in a second one, one must be sensible about these things. There are very few men of the right age that one might consider suitable who are not married or at best divorced.'

'Are you advising me to marry Shard?'

'I'm simply advising you not to do anything in haste—it would be in very bad taste to marry anyone in the near future. But it would be wise to stay friendly with Shard, and in time—well, who knows? Certainly there can be no harm in giving him a little mild encouragement while you get over things. Provided you don't do anything foolish, of course.'

'Like what?' Elise asked, still a little floored by all this.

'You're not a child, Elise,' her mother said impatiently. 'And neither is Shard. Like most men—I suspect, more than most—he isn't above going all out for whatever he can get with the least inconvenience to himself. He's over thirty now and hasn't married. Just make sure that he gives you a ring before you commit yourself.'

Elise didn't know what to say, but she felt a stinging warmth in her cheeks, as she turned her attention to distributing spoons on to saucers. She shouldn't, she supposed, be shocked by the candidness of her mother's speech, but she was. She had never realised before just how much money and social prestige meant to Katherine, although it had been the background to her entire life. For the first time she wondered how much her mother had influenced her own choice when she had married Peter.

When she handed Shard his cup, he looked at her keenly and asked, 'Is something wrong?'

Elise shook her head, surprised that her inner disturbance showed. As she made to move away, he caught her wrist in a warm grasp. 'Shall I take you home?' he asked softly.

She shook her head. 'I have my own car.'

'I'll ring you tomorrow.'

She remembered the lifting of her heart when she had learnt that he was repaying her grandfather's money, and realised that after all, there was no reason not to trust him. She lifted her head and smiled at him, almost gaily. 'Yes,' she said.

He released her and she moved away.

She saw her mother talking animatedly to him, later in the evening, and didn't miss the sardonic quality in his smile as he politely listened. But when he looked up and saw her watching from across the room, the smile changed, and she drew a quick little breath as the grey eyes seemed to kindle into warmth.

CHAPTER SIX

HIS voice came across the phone as vibrant as the man himself, and Elise felt her fingers tighten on the receiver as she spoke to him.

'See me tonight,' he said.

'Yes,' she answered. Then, consciously cool to hide the effect he had on her, she said, 'I'll give you a meal. It's time I proved I *can* cook—and I owe you several.'

His voice, too, sounded chilly as he replied. 'You owe me nothing. What time?'

She told him, and rang off, feeling as though she had burned some boats or something equally drastic. Which was ridiculous, she told herself. She had simply invited a man around for a meal in return for—she couldn't quite bring herself to use the word *kindness*. Kindness and Shard didn't go together, and yet surely there was no other way to describe his care of her lately? Still, she had an intuitive feeling that a phase was coming to an end.

When she opened the door to him there was nothing in his manner to confirm it. His eyes took in without haste the swept-up hairdo with the tiny tendrils carefully allowed to escape, the low-cut dress in soft voile, the single chunky metal bracelet that was her only ornament apart from Peter's rings. He didn't speak, and she simply stepped back, a smile of greeting on her lips, and let him in. She realised that Shard seldom bothered to say hello, as though the everyday words of greeting were superfluous between them.

He poured drinks for them while she piled vegetables into plates and placed them in the warming drawer of

the stove, and added finishing touches to a lamb casserole
in wine.

She came back into the small lounge and he handed
her a glass and moved over to a window, standing with
his back to it and watching her as she took a chair and
sipped at her drink.

He said, 'You're different.'

'Am I?' she asked. 'In what way?'

He didn't answer at once, his eyes regarding her with
cool, almost wary speculation. Then a slight, enigmatic
smile touched his mouth and he said. 'I'm not sure. Perhaps I will be—later.'

Elise said, half-mockingly, 'You don't change, Shard.'

'Would you like me to?'

She hesitated. 'That's a leading question. I have no
right to try and change you.'

Levelly, he said, 'You have any rights you choose to
claim.'

Her heart seemed to lurch, and she couldn't meet his
eyes, still less answer him.

Shard moved, and her nerves tensed, but he only came
to sit in the chair opposite. The silence lengthened, and
she had the impression that the tension it engendered
was deliberate, on his part. That he had stopped trying
to protect her from the currents that always ran between
them.

She finished her drink and went back to the kitchen,
glad to have the excuse to busy herself with serving up
the dinner.

They talked little over the meal, but when she had
cleared away the plates after the sweet kiwi-fruit dessert,
he took his coffee cup from her and said, 'You can cook.
The meal was delicious.'

Elise inclined her head and said demurely, 'Thank
you.'

He laughed softly, and she looked up, a smile on her lips, her eyes soft, and shining.

Shard put out a hand and touched a wisp of fair hair that lay gently on her cheek, and she felt his fingers like a lick of fire. She caught her lower lip briefly in her teeth and said, to dispel the moment, 'I finished my commission today.'

'The drawings for the book?'

'Yes.'

'I'd like to see them.'

She hesitated for a moment, suddenly afraid. Then she said, 'All right. I'll get them later.'

But when she went into the little spare room to fetch them, he followed, and looked at them there, as she took them out of the folio and spread them on the table where she worked.

He didn't touch any of them, but she saw him looking at them, one by one. He said, 'You've improved. They're very good.'

Then he looked up and said, 'This is Peter's child.'

'And mine,' she said. 'We lost him before he was born.'

The sudden pain that touched his eyes shocked her, even as she knew that her own eyes had filled with unexpected tears, and she felt Shard's arms about her, pulling her close.

She didn't cry any more, standing in the circle of his arms. She heard him say, 'I didn't know.'

'It was five years ago,' she said, her voice muffled against his shoulder. 'We tried again, but they said it might be impossible for me.'

Shard kept holding her without moving for a while longer. Then he lifted her face to his and kissed her, his mouth possessive, but more tender than she had ever known it.

They returned to the lounge, Shard's arm about her,

and sat on the sofa, her head resting against his shoulder.

Elise had put on a record some time ago, and it played through and then began again. She couldn't be bothered getting up to turn it over. She felt very happy, and when Shard said her name softly, she turned a smiling face up to him. He didn't kiss her again, but seemed to be trying to read her face, his eyes enigmatic.

She whispered, 'Shard?'

He said, his voice deep and steady, 'You're very amenable tonight.'

His finger traced the outline of her lips, and on impulse she kissed it. For a moment it stilled, and then moved again against her mouth, gently caressing. She put up a hand, catching his fingers and nuzzling her cheek against his palm.

'You didn't tell me,' she said, almost drowsily, 'that you were Cortland Construction.'

'Tell you? I thought you knew.'

She shook her head. 'Not until last night. My mother mentioned it.' She smiled. 'She thinks now,' she told him solemnly, 'that you might make a suitable son-in-law.'

She had expected that would amuse him, but when he began to laugh aloud, she sat away from him, staring. Because the laughter held a note of recklessness, a harsh undertone that went beyond bitterness and yet held that, too.

When he stopped, his lips still curved, but taut, his eyes glittering with an emotion she couldn't fathom, she looked at him uncertainly.

Shard leaned back, his eyes still holding that disturbing glitter as they slipped over the low-necked bodice of her flimsy dress, and she was reminded of the time years ago when he had come out of the house and watched her as she dived into the pool.

In protest, she turned away from him, but he caught

her shoulder and hauled her back into his arms, taking no notice of her short, futile resistance as his mouth found hers with devastating precision and passion, pushing her head back into the curve of his shoulder and arm, insistently opening her lips to an implacable sensual invasion.

This time there was no tenderness and no compassion in the way he held her, his arms imprisoned her inescapably. His kiss was not a comforting caress but an arrogant demand, and when she stopped struggling against him he wasn't satisfied with mere passivity. She held out as long as she could against the dizzying waves of excitement that seemed to wash over her, some part of her still resisting his power over her emotions, wanting to deny him the victory. But her response, when at last he drew it from her, was complete and perfect. The fiercely independent satisfaction of denying him was replaced by the knowledge of the pleasure she could give him, that was equal to the pleasure that he gave her. And also by the knowledge that for neither of them was it enough.

When at last he let her go he did it suddenly and with an effort, standing abruptly and going to the window, pulling aside the curtain and standing with his hand clenched on the fabric, his shoulders hunched a little forward as the thumb of the other hand hooked into his belt.

Her fingers trying to cool the fire in her cheeks, Elise felt a quick surge of triumph. Shard was not quite in control, for once, and she was was glad because it was she who had done that to him.

She touched her hair, amazed that the pinned-up style seemed still in place, and arranged her legs neatly, ankles to one side and tucked together in a pose of conscious grace. She stopped her fingers trembling by clasping them

together on her lap, at first tightly and then carefully loosened. And she moistened her stinging mouth with her tongue and put her lips firmly and precisely together.

Still with his back to her, Shard said, 'We can be married next week.'

She felt as though something had been thrown at her very hard. Then a strange mixture of emotions, longing, despair, fear and anger shot through her. She knew that she wanted desperately to marry Shard, but was acutely aware that he had never spoken a word of love to her, and his calm assumption that she would submit to his unconventional haste both frightened and infuriated her.

'No,' she protested. 'I can't——'

He turned then, his eyes and mouth hard.

She said, 'Not so soon, Shard—I couldn't.'

His slight smile was cruel. 'On the contrary, you've just proved rather conclusively that you could.'

Her face flamed. 'I didn't mean that! It just wouldn't be decent for me to rush into marriage less than six months after my husband's death——'

'You mean it isn't socially acceptable,' he said. 'Supposing I agreed to wait—I take it six months is the proper minimum for mourning—would you marry me then?'

'Yes.'

He looked at her almost with curiosity, the coldness in his eyes chilling her. 'If you had a good reason——' he said. 'But you haven't. You've taken six years from us, Elise. I won't let you have any more just to satisfy the so-called decent feelings of a lot of people who have nothing to do with us. Next week—or never.'

Her lips parted in dismay. She couldn't believe that he meant it—and she saw that he did. She saw that if she refused Shard would write her out of his life as someone who had not, after all, been worth the feeling he had had for her. Someone who thought more of conventional social mores than she did of him.

And she also saw that he knew what a refusal would mean to her, how much she wanted him, and that his ultimatum was calculated to make her tacitly admit it.

Hating him for that, but loving him too much to accept a life without him, she moved her hands in a little gesture of pleading. 'Shard, couldn't you——'

'No. Next week, Elise.'

She looked at the hard jut of his jaw, the uncompromising set of his mouth, and the almost imperceptible movement of a small muscle on his jawline. He was not certain of her capitulation, and for a moment she relished that tiny hint of uncertainty, her only small revenge.

Then she said, 'Very well, Shard. Next week.'

The muscle in his jaw relaxed, although his eyes contained no warmth. 'I'll make the arrangements,' he said.

She stood up as he walked to the door, following him. With his hand on the latch he turned to look at her, and she stopped, three feet away. His gaze went to her hair, and he asked, 'Is that pinned?'

'Yes.'

'I've a good mind to unpin it and let it down.'

'Don't you like it?'

He almost smiled, a brief warmth showing in his eyes. 'I like it very much—because it makes me want to take it down. Wear it like that for our wedding.'

Elise had expected a brief, businesslike register office ceremony, but they were married in a church. She had not been consulted, but as the day unfolded she realised that Shard had arranged everything just as she would have wanted it. The church was small and there were flowers, but not too many. She knew the minister, but he was not the one who had officiated when she married Peter. There were no guests, only her parents and grandfather and Gary, who had flown up from Wellington to be present. His wife had elected to stay home with their children.

Her hand felt strange when she removed Peter's rings that morning, and she was a little strung-up until she felt Shard slip his own gold band on in their place, his fingers warm and sure as they held her hand. She looked fleetingly up into his face then, and found it remote and darkly shuttered. But when he met her eyes, his seemed to soften a little, and his hand tightened on hers for a brief moment.

Afterwards they were all taken to a restaurant for a meal with champagne but no wedding cake, for which Elise was thankful. And when her father cleared his throat and began to push back his chair, Shard put a hand on his arm and said quietly, 'No speeches, please, Howard. We'll accept a quiet toast, if you care to propose it.'

As they drove northward to the quiet little beach where Shard had taken a house for the next ten days, she said, 'You had no friends there.'

'Gary and your grandfather are friends of mine.'

'It was—nice,' she said. 'Thank you.'

Shard glanced at her and said nothing, his face unreadable.

'I've never met any of your friends,' she reminded him.

'Do you want to?'

'Of course I do. I'm your wife——'

He said, 'Yes.'

The sudden panic that gripped her then was ridiculous, she told herself; merely, surely, a belated case of bridal nerves. Shard was driving steadily, his eyes fixed on the road ahead as it wound away from the harbour and into the hills of the North Shore with its panoramic suburbia of houses and trees. There was nothing in that single flat affirmative to make her feel trapped—threatened and as though she had run into a blind alley that held no possibility of escape, while some dark pursuer stalked her.

The road wound into the cool serenity of native bush, and out again through Albany with its pseudo-Tudor hotel building, and she was still gripped by a paralysing sense of unreasoning fear. Her nails dug into clammy palms in her lap, her eyes stared unseeing at the green undulations of the passing countryside until they ached. And Shard drove on in calm silence.

When he stopped at Orewa, drawing up on smooth grass overlooking the long sweep of sand and said, 'Like to stretch your legs and have a drink?' she almost gulped with relief at the mundane suggestion. Seeming not to notice her tension, he bought them orange juice in paper cups, and then they strolled for half an hour along the firm, damp sand, watching the wide waves ripple gently to the shore.

They walked two feet apart, and when another couple passed them, hand in hand as their bare feet kicked up little splashes in the edges of the waves, she glanced at Shard with a question in her eyes.

His mouth moved in a grim little smile, and he took a hand from his pocket and thrust it out, reading her mind, waiting for her to take it.

But as she did, his fingers closed on her wrist, and though they walked back to the car side by side, her shoulder touching his arm, it was as though she was his prisoner, his hard fingers on her wrist like a shackle.

The small house stood on a shallow rise overlooking the sea as it rushed impetuously into a pretty little cove. Coarse grasses tried to push their way through the sand to form a rough lawn, and in one corner of the fenced section two trees of an indeterminate genus were battling the sea breezes that had bent them out of shape. The house was low and built of weathered wood, with long windows to the sea and a wide terrace linking the bedroom and the living room with the outdoors. At first, inside and out, it seemed plain and almost starkly functional, but the chairs were deep and comfortable, the rugs of natural wool contrasted pleasantly with the satiny texture of stained floorboards, and the small kitchen had every amenity, while the bathroom was discreetly luxurious.

In the bedroom, while Shard was fetching their cases from the car, Elise put down her bag and the smart make-up case that her mother had given her on the built-in dressing table, took in the view of the sea through the ranch-sliders to the terrace, and glanced quickly away from the wide, deep-mattressed bed with its hand-woven cover. The mirror showed her green eyes looking huge and darker than usual, a face slightly pale but composed, her hair still prettily in place. She still wore the new dress she had bought for the wedding, a narrow-waisted, almost plain dress that was without frills or ornament, but of a soft and silky material that clung where it touched and flowed where it didn't. The colour was a muted green that softened the colour of her eyes, giving them a misty and mysterious look.

She heard Shard coming back into the house, and before she could return to the living room he was in the doorway.

She couldn't look at him, fumbling in her bag for a comb, pretending that she needed it and was too preoccupied to notice him. But she knew that he had put down the cases and had moved to stand behind her. Then she felt his hands on her shoulders, and his lips touched the nape of her neck, where the swept-up hairstyle exposed it. She had the comb in her hand, and her fingers tightened, the teeth digging into the flesh of her palm.

His mouth moved over her skin seductively, then lifted. And his hands moved, slowly pulling the pins from her hair until it tumbled round her shoulders.

Elise stood perfectly still, her head still bent, until his arms came round her and he took her wrist in one hand and prised the comb away with the other. Her hand came open and there was a row of tiny marks across the centre of her palm, and two pinprick drops of blood.

Shard pulled her round to face him, his eyes fixed on her hand, then raised to stare into hers. His voice rough, he said, 'You little fool! What are you afraid of?'

Of you, she thought, but it wasn't in her to admit it.

His hand tightened on her wrist, and she knew that he didn't know it. Almost savagely he said, 'I told you, you have any rights you care to claim. That includes the right to say no.'

Her lips parted in sheer astonishment, and he stepped back, releasing her wrist to pivot on his heel and leave the room. Elise heard him locking up the car, and wondered if it was necessary in this remote spot, or if he had made it an excuse to leave her alone for a few minutes.

The right to say no—of course she had that right, but it was a right a strong man could easily disregard, and that in law was not even recognised between husband and wife. But Shard had told her he would respect it— and any other rights she claimed. Deliberately he had placed himself in her power, unafraid. Shard was strong enough to do that. She didn't know if she was strong enough to cope with it.

She went into the kitchen and began opening cupboards, finding frozen supplies in the refrigerator, deliberately setting her mind to working out a menu for their first meal.

She refused his help, and he leaned against the door jamb and watched her as she prepared a meal of chops and frozen vegetables and a bean salad. She didn't mind him watching her, she felt her own movements as though she could see herself through his eyes, deft and quick, and was conscious of enjoying his lazily appreciative surveillance.

They didn't talk as they ate, the breakers hurling into the cove outside providing a background that was both exciting and hypnotic, broken occasionally by the soft thud of a moth or huhu beetle flinging itself against the lighted windows.

Elise made coffee and then Shard pushed her into an armchair and said, 'Rest. I'll wash up.'

She let him, but after a few minutes she slid back the glass doors and went out, enjoying the sharp salty scent of the sea and the clear roll and swish of the waves, dimly glimpsed in the darkness as brief flashes of moving white.

Shard finished his task and joined her, leaning against the low wooden railing beside her.

'Would you like to walk?' he asked.

'Yes.' She went back into the house, peeled off her tights and dropped them into a drawer, found a soft wool wrap for her shoulders and, leaving her shoes where she had kicked them off, rejoined Shard.

'You have a gypsy look,' he said softly as she paused beside him. 'Out of character, but intriguing.'

She thought she caught a note of mockery, and without speaking she stepped lightly down from the terrace to the springy grass, and through the gap in the fence where no one had bothered to erect a gate, until her bare feet trod on cool loose sand.

Shard had followed swiftly and strode beside her on to firmer sand near the waterline, the evening breeze lifting his hair and tugging at the opened collar of his white shirt. Elise lifted her face to feel the wind, putting up her hand to brush a strand of her hair away from her eyes. The woollen shawl about her shoulders slipped without her restraining hand, and Shard caught it and readjusted it for her. Then he took his hand away and they walked side by side in the darkness until they reached the great outcropping rock that marked the end of the cove.

Surefooted even in darkness, Elise clambered up on to the smooth shelf of rock that jutted into the water, dropping the shawl carelessly on the bare ground, and sank on to it, hugging her knees, her eyes looking wide into the dark sea.

Shard stood beside her, his legs braced slightly apart. Her shoulder almost touched his knee, but he didn't move closer or sit down beside her.

'I love the sea,' she said.

'I know.'

'That's why you brought me here, isn't it?' she said softly. 'Because you knew.'

'Yes.'

This whole day, he had been laying his gifts to her at her feet. It should have been a triumph. But instead she found herself afraid. Afraid—but excited, like someone engaging in an exhilarating but dangerous sport, using potentially lethal weapons. It was tempting to use the weapon he had given her, to test her power over him.

She stood up and stepped back, leaving the white triangle of her wrap spread on the rock, the breeze lifting the corners. Shard turned his head to look at her, and she looked straight back.

The shawl lifted completely at one corner and folded

over itself. And Shard stooped and picked it up.

Without a word she turned, scooping her hair forward with her hand, and waited for him. She felt the lightness of the wool about her shoulders, and then he was ahead of her, jumping lithely down on to the sand, standing there to wait for her.

He didn't offer his hand and she didn't ask for it, but when she landed on a half-buried, unseen rock and painfully turned her ankle, he swooped forward instantly, catching her up against his body and holding her for a long moment.

When she stirred he let her go at once, keeping only a consciously light hold on her arm. 'Are you all right?' he asked her.

'Yes.' Her ankle throbbed, but she could walk on it. The pain would soon recede. She took his arm and leaned on it a little as they walked back across the sand to where the lights still gleamed at them out of the darkness. Elise suddenly felt very confident and elated. Shard had scared her with his apparent aloofness and icy control, his enigmatic expression and his harshness even as he promised her immunity from any threat of violence. But when he had held her for that short space of time in his arms, she had felt the way his fingers closed tightly on her shoulder, his swiftly drawn breath against her temple, the unmistakable stirring of his desire. Shard was, after all, very much a man.

She showered off the gritty sand that clung to her feet and legs, and pulled on a new nylon silk wrap, simple and clinging like her wedding dress, but more revealing. Shard was in the living room as she came out, but as she stood in the bedroom taking out the pins that had held her hair while she showered, he came in and took some things from his bag and went into the bathroom.

She brushed out her hair and went to stand by the

window, a small phial of perfume in her hand. She dabbed some on her finger, looking out through a narrow gap in the curtains at the distant occasional flashes of white that was all she could see of the ocean. She ran a perfume-moistened finger down the line of her throat to the hollow between her breasts, and slowly replaced the cap. The bathroom door opened, and she put down the perfume on the window ledge.

Shard walked quietly, but she knew when he came to stand in the doorway and, still with her back to him, she reached up and closed the curtain.

She knew that she wasn't going to say no.

CHAPTER SEVEN

THEY lay on the beach after a swim, Elise with her hand on Shard's shoulder while his fingers played with her hair.

'You've sand in it,' he said.

'I'll have to shower it out,' she answered drowsily. Overhead the sky was an intense blue. It was all she could see, and all she wanted was to keep looking at it while Shard's arm was about her and his hands touched her skin and her hair.

'I've always wanted to see you like this,' he told her.

'Like what?'

'Tousled and undressed.'

'A bikini is not undress,' she informed him, turning her cheek against his bare skin.

'It wouldn't take much——' he said, his hands moving insinuatingly.

'Shard—no!' she protested, trying to wriggle away from him. 'Not here!'

'There's no one about.'

'Someone might come along.'

'So?' He had turned so that she lay in his arms, his head shadowing her face.

'We can't—I can't!' she hastily amended, as she saw his eyebrows lift, and his hand moved to the fastening at her back. 'Please, Shard!'

He moved, and stood up, his shadow falling across her as she stared up at him, her breathing still unsteady.

'Get up,' he said. 'We'll go back to the house.'

*

'These sheets will have to be changed now,' she said later. 'They're full of sand.'

'We could have stayed on the beach. Don't pull the sheet up—I like looking at you.'

'Am I "tousled and undressed" enough for you now?'

He leaned over and she felt his lips on her shoulder. 'You're beautiful,' he said. 'You always were.'

'Even when I was being bitchy to you?'

Shard laughed softly against her skin. 'Especially then.'

'You always laughed. It was as though you enjoyed it.'

He raised his head and looked at her, his eyes alight. 'Of course I did—it proved that you weren't indifferent, no matter how desperately you tried to pretend.'

'I had to pretend. I was engaged to Peter.'

His eyes hardened. They had been married for three days, and this was the first time Peter's name had been mentioned.

He said, his voice harsh, 'Engagements have been broken.'

'You don't understand.' She hesitated, wondering if she could explain to him the doubts and bewilderment she had felt when she was only eighteen years old.

But he didn't give her a chance. His mouth had an ugly twist to it, and he rolled off the bed and stood up, not looking at her. 'I understand all right,' he said, and turned his back on her, walking off to the bathroom.

Elise was careful not to mention Peter again during the days of their honeymoon. One day, she hoped, Shard might be willing to tolerate listening to her reasons for rushing into that impetuous marriage with Peter. But she supposed no man would relish a discussion of his predecessor on his honeymoon. Besides, she wasn't sure just how much she could reveal. Peter, after all, must be entitled to some reticence on her part, some loyalty to his memory.

If it imposed some strain on their relationship, Shard appeared not to notice. He made love to her with the same intense concentration and frank enjoyment as before, and with the same sensual satisfaction in watching her abandon herself to the pleasure he gave her. She knew that she was finding heights with him that with Peter she had never attained, and was bothered by a nagging guilt about it that she did her best to curb. Common sense said that it was futile and unconstructive to dwell on the past when the future was so full of promise.

But just now they lived from day to day with a completeness that Elise realised was almost abnormal, so consciously did they enter into it. They seldom spoke of anything but each other and their present surroundings, they bought no newspapers and ignored the colour television set in the lounge of the house. There was no mail. Once she asked Shard if anyone in Cortland Construction knew where they were. He said, 'They can find me if the end of the world comes. They've instructions not to, otherwise.' It was as though they had a tacit pact by which, for them, the past and the world had ceased to exist.

'How did you find this place?' she asked him one evening as they sat on the terrace, watching the dying sun colour the water with a shimmer of gold.

'I stayed here once, with the owner. He designed the place.'

'An architect?'

'Yes. You like it, don't you?'

'Very much.'

'Shall I buy it?'

She turned to look at him, seeing he was serious. 'Would he sell?'

Shard shrugged. 'Most people will sell anything if the price is right.'

'I've never heard you cynical before,' she commented.

'It comes with experience.' His face looked remote and hard.

'Perhaps——' she hesitated.

'Yes?'

'Would he design a house for us?'

'It's his job. Is that what you'd like?'

'Wouldn't you?' But she knew she shouldn't have asked him that. Whenever she expressed a preference, a wish, he would go along with it. But he seldom committed himself to a preference of his own. It was as though he wanted nothing but whatever would make her happy.

He said, 'I'll see him when we get back.'

On their last night they swam in the darkness and made love afterwards on the cool sand, and even though its grittiness clung to their damp limbs their pleasure in each other seemed intensified by the salt-tangled night that enfolded them and the near, insistent, steady booming of the waves.

Late into the night they stood on the terrace, with Shard's arms holding her back against him and his cheek against her hair, looking at the scattered stars beyond high wind-borne clouds and saying nothing.

After a long time Shard lifted the hair that lay, still damp from swimming and the shower, against her nape, and put his lips to the warm skin beneath. Elise dipped her head, smiling, and his hands tightened against her waist, then moved lightly over her body. When his mouth left her, she tipped back her head against his shoulder and gave her mouth to his, until he turned her

into his arms, and then lifted her to carry her inside to
the bed.

Shard's flat was a little bigger than hers, the living room
large enough for entertaining, and the spare bedroom
which she took over for her studio, roomier too than the
small one she had used before. The place was modern
and expensively furnished, but there was something
starkly masculine about it, excepting for the double bed
in the main bedroom which was covered in an old-gold
satin spread. Elise didn't ask it it was new.

'Make what changes you like,' Shard told her. 'I can
pay for them.'

She made few, only adding a few softening touches in
the way of cushions and bowls of flowers, and a couple
of less angular-looking chairs.

She asked him, 'Do you want me to be a stay-at-home
wife? I've had the offer of another commission—this one
is for a textbook.'

'Do what *you* want,' he said. 'Would you prefer a job
that takes you away from the house?'

'No. I like working on my own. You don't mind if I
take the commission?'

Looking slightly impatient, he said, 'I don't mind.'

Faintly chilled, Elise wondered if he would be glad she
had something to occupy her. Shard didn't bring home
business colleagues often, as Peter had, expecting his wife
to be on hand to entertain them. And when they went
out it was usually on their own, not to some business
dinner or the kind of semi-business social function that
she had been used to.

She told him she would like to invite her parents for
dinner and he said, 'Of course.' She mentioned a date and
he glanced at the calendar and said, 'Yes, okay.'

When they came he was suavely polite, parrying Katherine's one or two barbs easily, and to add insult to injury, almost absentmindedly; and treated Howard's queries about Cortland Construction and his remarks on world affairs and business with courteous attention. It struck Elise that he was like a man playing a part on stage, saying lines that he had learnt by heart.

As she went to the bedroom with her mother to fetch the coat and bag Kate had left there, the older woman said, 'Well, marriage appears to have mellowed him. Congratulations, Elise. I do think you might have waited a little longer, for decency's sake, but——'

'Shard wouldn't wait, Mother.'

Katherine laughed. 'My dear, of course he would have waited, if you'd insisted. Don't you realise you have him on a string? He agrees with every slightest suggestion you make.'

Elise knew that he did, but—'No one ever had Shard on a string, Mother,' she said with conviction.

'Of course, it can't last,' her mother said with hard practicality. 'If you're wise you'll make the best of it while it does. Men are perfect fools when they're in love, but they're also inclined to fall for the superficial qualities a girl has. You're young and pretty now, but it takes more than that to hold a man after the first year or two. It's a pity you can't have children.'

Elise paled. 'It isn't certain,' she said.

'No, but——' Katherine's face was easy to read. After five years it seemed unlikely. She shrugged and picked up her bag. 'Well, there are other ways,' she said as they moved out again into the hall. 'You were a credit to Peter, and I'm sure Shard will find you an asset to him, as well, once you begin entertaining. Of course, it's wise for you to continue to live rather quietly for a few more months——'

Shard and Howard were coming out of the lounge, Howard turning to speak to the other man. Elise didn't know if Shard had heard what her mother was saying. He glanced up at them, but his expression didn't alter as he saw the guests out.

He followed Elise into the lounge later, and watched as she collected coffee cups and glasses and straightened the new cushions. Her mother had said, 'Shard will find you an asset to him——' But she was sure that he wasn't interested in her capabilities as a hostess, and her attempts to show an interest in the business had been deflected with unmistakable firmness. Sometimes she felt that she was somehow wandering, without guidelines. Marriage to Peter had been comparatively easy. She had been young and inexperienced, but Peter had been clear about what was expected of her, and with her mother as a model she had managed to live up to that. What Shard expected of her she wasn't sure. He didn't seem to have any need of her help, understanding or advice. And her mother had with devastating frankness put into words her own unease about Shard's attitude. That he found her sexually exciting, she knew; he was and always had been very candid about that. If she ceased to attract him in that way, *could* she hold him? She could not forget that even in their most intimate moments she had never heard him say that he loved her.

She picked up the small tray on which she had piled the cups and glasses, and Shard stood aside to let her pass and take them to the kitchen.

'Shall I help?' he asked as she passed him. Elise shook her head. She just left the things on the draining board and seeing that Shard had switched off the lounge lights, went into their bedroom.

He was standing in the middle of the room, apparently doing nothing, and there was a wry twist to his mouth.

He looked up as Elise came in, and began undoing his shirt.

She walked over to him and hooked her arms about his neck, and his hands left the buttons and lightly clasped her waist. Elise nuzzled her head under his chin and put her lips briefly to his skin where the collar of his shirt opened. She leaned back against his hands and said, looking into his face, 'Shard, let's have a party.'

His eyes held amusement and something else that she couldn't define, and she was suddenly certain that he had heard her mother's parting remark.

'Sure,' he said. 'Who do you want to invite?'

'All our friends,' she said. 'Yours and mine. I haven't met any of your friends.'

She suddenly thought that the other thing in his eyes was wariness. 'You may not like them,' he told her.

'Why not?'

'Some of them are not the kind of people who get invited to your mother's parties.'

Elise flushed and moved away from him. 'This isn't my mother's party,' she said stiffly. 'It's ours.'

'Okay,' he shrugged. 'I'll give you a list.' He was looking at her intently, and she asked:

'What's the matter?'

'Just one thing,' he said. 'I won't have my friends invited to my home and then patronised or put down. So don't do it, honey.'

A bright flame of anger seemed to shoot through her. Almost choking with it, she managed a muffled, 'Thanks a lot!' and turned to go into the bathroom, shutting the door decisively.

When she got into bed and put out the light, he touched her turned shoulder and she hunched away from him, muttering, 'I'm tired.'

'You're sulking,' he said, and turned her to face him, pressing her head into the pillow with his kiss.

She tried to push him away, and he caught her hands and held them while he went on kissing her. When he stopped, she said, 'You told me I could say no.'

'Sure you can.' But his mouth was on hers again, persuading, probing, until her body lost its stiffness and her lips opened to his passion.

Then he lifted his head and said, 'Goodnight, Elise,' and moved away to his own side of the bed.

Elise lay rigid, biting her lip hard, burning with humiliation and anger. Shard had done it deliberately to punish her. He would fall in with her every suggestion, give her anything she asked for. But nobody had Shard on a string.

The party was not a big one. The list Shard had given her wasn't long, and she tried to match the number of her own friends to it. That wasn't difficult because in the main she invited people who had known her before she met Peter. Most of the friends she had made since, she realised, had been more Peter's than hers.

Looking around the room half-way through the evening, she thought it was relatively easy to distinguish her friends from Shard's. Hers tended to be of the same mould, pretty, well-groomed young women accompanied by nice men with 'young executive' stamped invisibly on their confident features and their impeccable clothes. Shard's friends included an elderly man who told her he was a retired engineer, a middle-aged couple who said Shard had boarded with them years before, and an enormous Maori man with a paralysing handshake and a fruity deep voice which announced to anyone interested, 'I'm Matt. Yeah I work for this joker——' jerking his head in Shard's direction with a cheerful grin. His wife was a beautiful, delicate-looking young woman who stayed quietly in her husband's considerable shadow.

'Who is he?' Elise whispered to Shard when she got the chance. 'He looks like a bulldozer driver.'

Shard grinned down at her, his eyes gleaming and narrow. 'Right first time,' he told her. 'And one of the best in the business.'

He introduced her to a smiling, fair man and said, 'This is Cole Finlay, Elise. He's agreed to design a house for us.'

She had almost thought that was a part of their honeymoon that belonged to the dream world they had inhabited then, but apparently Shard had not forgotten.

'I hear you like my beach house, Mrs Cortland,' the architect said. 'We'll all have to get together sometime and I'll find out just what you want. Shard tells me it's entirely up to you, but I'd like to have him in on the planning.'

'So would I,' she agreed. 'And please call me Elise. Perhaps you might come and have dinner with us next week, and we could discuss it then? And Mrs Finlay?'

'There's no Mrs Finlay,' he told her. 'I'll be on my own, if that's okay.'

Couples had been dancing in a small cleared space in one corner of the room, but the record player suddenly gave a despairing whine and stopped in the middle of a disc. The dancers gathered round the player in mock-dismay, and someone called, 'Is there an electrician in the house?'

Apparently there was, for there were laughing cries of 'Where's Gabe?' and a lanky young man ambled over to the group, parked a half-full glass on a nearby table and stooped to inspect the apparatus, encouraged by helpful comments from the concerned watchers, who included Shard, leaning on the wall and looking more relaxed than Elise had ever seen him as he grinned back at some joking advice not to let Gabe touch his expensive stereo gear.

'Mrs Cortland——' said a voice at her elbow. She turned to a tall dark-haired man with a long face which was given an elfish air by his triangular smile.

'Yes, Mr——?' she hesitated, trying to fit his name to the face.

'Call me Don,' he said. 'The bar is deserted. Let me get you a drink while the crisis develops.'

She laughed and followed him to the table near the kitchen that held the drinks. 'My name's Elise,' she said, as he poured her gin and lime for her. 'Do you work with Shard?'

'No, I manage a factory. Shard did some construction work for us recently when we put up a building to house some new plant. But we met some years ago when we both received our management diplomas in the same year.'

She hadn't known Shard had one. 'It's a correspondence course, isn't it?' she asked.

'Correspondence or night school. Shard was a tiger for punishment. I think he was studying for engineering qualifications at the same time. And working in the daytime, of course. Not pushing a pen, either. He knows the construction business inside and out.'

'So it wasn't just money——' she murmured.

'Lord, no! Money and know-how and the ability to find good men and keep them. I've talked to some of the guys who work for him, and they reckon he's all right. He's tough and not chummy, but they know where they are, and if they do the job right he'll give them a fair deal. Otherwise, it's out on their ear.'

Elise smiled a little wistfully. 'You know, I've learned a lot about my husband tonight.'

Shard came up to them then, slipping his arm about her waist, saying, 'The record player's fixed. Dance with me.'

She went into his arms on the improvised dance floor, and relaxed against him. 'It's a good party,' she said.

'Yes. Thank you, Elise.'

She lifted her head and said, 'I like your friends.'

His answering glance was enigmatic, and she said, rather hurt, 'You didn't expect me to, did you?'

'I didn't know,' he said. Then he smiled. 'They like you, too. I've been receiving compliments on my choice all night.'

'I've had one or two as well,' she said demurely, and he laughed and pulled her closer.

When they had all gone, she half-lay against the sofa cushions, eyes almost closed.

'Tired?' Shard asked as he returned from seeing the last couple to their car.

'Mmm. I can't be bothered going to bed,' she said.

He laughed softly, and bent, swinging her easily into his arms.

Her arms hung loosely round his neck as he carried her to the bedroom and laid her down. He undid her zip and eased off her dress, and pulled the covers of the bed up over her shoulders. She felt his lips brush her temple, and fell instantly asleep.

CHAPTER EIGHT

SHARD came home early from work one day and said, 'Put on something tough and sensible. I want to show you something.'

Elise had started cooking their meal, but something that was taut and alive in his face stopped her voicing any protest. She turned off the stove and went into the bedroom to find jeans and sneakers and a cotton shirt.

Shard drove out of the city to where the road wound around the hills above the Manukau Harbour on the western side, and kept going until they had almost reached the Waitakeres. Then he took them down a winding side road and through a farm gate, past a square, wide-verandahed old kauri farmhouse, and eventually into a cleared space among stands of totara, tawa and kanuka interspersed with tree ferns and other native plants. The land sloped gently to a cliff face covered with taupata and clinging vines and plants, and the blue sea lapped at its foot.

'Would you like to live here?' Shard asked her.

It was perfect, and she said so. 'But you——' she said. 'You'll have to travel and it's out of town.'

Shard shrugged. 'It's less than an hour.'

They walked to where the cliff face fell to the sea, and he said, 'I've got an option on it. Do you want it?'

Elise knew better than to say, *do you?* If she wanted it, it was hers—or theirs.

'You spoil me, Shard,' she said softly. 'More than my father ever did. I always thought—that you felt it would do me good to go without, and you're always giving me things.'

'I'm trying to keep you in the manner to which you've been accustomed,' he said mockingly.

'Why?' She turned to face him, her steady gaze a challenge.

His smile was twisted, unreadable. 'Because it pleases me.'

'To give me everything I want?'

'Yes.'

Groping for an understanding of his motives, she asked hesitantly, 'Is it important, to keep me in my accustomed style?'

Rather gently he replied, 'It is to you.' Then abruptly he turned back towards the car and said, 'I'll send Cole out to look at the land before he comes to discuss the house with us.'

She began, 'Shard——'

But he might not have heard. He pushed her firmly into the passenger seat and closed the door, and as he slid into his own seat he was saying, 'You asked Cole to come to dinner, didn't you?'

'Yes, I thought some time next week, but haven't set a day with him yet. Shard——'

'I'll see him,' he said. 'Would Tuesday be okay?'

'Yes. Any day next week is fine.'

'You'd better have some ideas ready for him, then. Have you thought about the sort of house you want?'

Defeated, she said, 'Not very much. Perhaps something rather like the beach house. I expect we should take his advice on a lot of things.'

'Not if you don't like it.'

'No,' she said with irony, 'of course not.' Shard would never for a moment be tempted to take advice unless he saw very good reasons for following it. Which made it all the more puzzling that he was always so ready to fall in with her every whim. It seemed ridiculous to be uneasy about it, but she was. And yet the core of her unease was something even more intangible. She felt that something was missing in their relationship but was unable to name it. At times there seemed about their marriage an air of unreality as though it was a dream from which she knew there would one day be an abrupt and frightening awakening. There was about Shard a deeprooted, hard self-sufficiency that she was aware had been part of his attraction in the beginning of their relationship, that sometimes bruised her when she made attempts at emotional intimacy and found her efforts coolly rebuffed. In the physical sphere nothing was withheld, their joy in each other complete and unrestrained. But that only strengthened her deep awareness that in Shard's mind and emotions there was a deliberate invisible line drawn beyond which he would not permit her to intrude.

Cole Finlay came to dinner and afterwards they sat over coffee at the table, and he took out a sketch pad and notebook.

'Tell me first what you want,' he said. 'Apart from the usual offices and a lounge overlooking the sea, which I'm assuming——'

'Will you want your studio to have a sea view, Elise?' Shard asked her.

'Studio?'

'Shard tells me you're an artist, Elise,' said Cole. 'You'll need a studio with a good light, of course, and perhaps a view for inspiration?'

Elise laughed. 'I'm an illustrator, in a small way,' she said. 'I use the spare bedroom. I hadn't really thought of a studio.'

'Of course you'll have a studio,' Shard said.

Cole wrote down something in his notebook. 'Now, bedrooms,' he said. 'The main bedroom with its own bathroom suite?'

Shard nodded, and Cole's pen was busy again. 'Guest room?' He glanced up, scribbled happily again. 'Children's rooms—or future provision for, perhaps?'

'No children's rooms,' Shard said harshly.

The silence was sharp and intense. Cole's pen remained poised and he didn't look up. 'No children's rooms,' he repeated matter-of-factly. 'Will you need an office at home, Shard?'

'Yes,' said Elise.

Cole made a note. 'Brings work home, does he?' he murmured affably.

Shard had never brought work home. But Elise said pleasantly, 'I think Shard would like a private retreat, where he can be alone.'

She knew Shard was looking at her across the table, but she wouldn't meet his eyes. 'He likes to shut himself away sometimes,' she went on. 'From—everything.'

Cole looked up with a smile. 'He's lucky to have such an understanding wife. Most men like a private place, but some women complain.'

'Oh—do they?' she asked with cool surprise. 'I'll get some more coffee.' And she took the cups and got up to escape Shard's eyes.

Several hours later, she lay against Shard's shoulder in the big bed, his fingers tangling gently in her spread hair.

Into the darkness, he asked, 'What makes you feel I want to shut you out?'

For a moment she held her breath. If they could talk about it, perhaps the barriers could be removed ...

Carefully, she said, 'Isn't that what you're doing, when

you won't talk about things?'

'Such as?'

'Your work, for one thing. You choked me off when I tried to ask you about it.'

Shard was silent for several moments. Finally he said, 'Were you really interested, or just being the dutiful wife? I thought you were asking because it's expected of you to take some mild interest in your husband's business.'

'If I was,' she said, 'is there anything wrong with that?'

'Yes. Whatever you give me, I want it to be freely given, not as part of your duty as you see it.'

'It wasn't that,' she said. 'I remember how you used to talk about construction work before—when——' When they used to meet before she married Peter. But she couldn't say that. 'You made it sound exciting and interesting. I liked listening to you.'

Again there was a silence, and the shoulder that pillowed her head seemed to tense a little. 'Then it wasn't entirely a basic animal instinct?' he said. 'Biological chemistry?'

She remembered flinging those words at him, years ago. 'No,' she said. 'I don't think I believed that even then, entirely. But that aspect was so strong, it did tend to swamp the rest—I think it frightened me. And you said some pretty harsh things too, that night. Did you really think that I'd deliberately led you on, tried to make you propose, for the pleasure of turning you down?'

'It fitted.'

She stirred against him in soft protest. 'No,' she said. 'I was never the sophisticated little tease that you seemed to imagine. I was young and confused. No one had ever made me feel the way you did, and you were so—so different. And there was Peter who loved me and needed me.'

'And made you feel safe.'

'Perhaps—that, too,' she acknowledged. 'Do you despise me for that? I suppose there was a lot of truth in the things you said the night we went out in my car, that first time. I had lived a fairly sheltered life, and been cushioned from most shocks. But it wasn't all selfishness, Shard. My parents were keen on my marrying Peter, and I'd made a promise to him. It wasn't only that I was afraid for myself, afraid that my physical feelings for you were warping my judgment, afraid, too, that you weren't as honest as you seemed. It was also the fear of hurting people—Peter, my parents—you don't have any family, perhaps you can't understand, but I'd been brought up to think of how my actions affected them, to care about their feelings. I know my family aren't perfect, but I love them.'

'Love——'

'You said once you have no use for it,' she said, her voice a little unsteady. 'Is that still how you feel?'

'If that's love,' he said, 'I want no part of it.'

She was quiet, staring into the darkness. 'You haven't forgiven me,' she said. 'You've never forgiven me for marrying Peter. Did I hurt you very much?'

'You hurt me very much. But that needs no forgiveness. What I can't take is that you hurt yourself. You weren't what they tried to make you, but you made yourself conform to their pattern. You had guts— courage and willpower, and you perverted them——'

'Perverted?' she queried.

'Yes. You should have used them to become the person you wanted to be, to do what you wanted to do, not to force yourself into a role that was set for you by other people.'

'But that's selfish!' she exclaimed, shocked.

'Is it? What gave them the right to ask you to deform yourself to fit their expectations? The only rights a person has over another are those that are freely given. The only duties they have are those that are freely accepted. Anything else is coercion, and coercion isn't fit to go by the name of love. It isn't a fit transaction for human beings.'

'I chose it,' she said slowly. And then—'I wasn't unhappy.'

'No—just less happy than you might have been. And less complete, and less free.'

'Am I free now—married to you?'

'If you're not, it's because you don't want to be.'

Elise wasn't sure what he meant by that.

At breakfast Shard asked casually, 'Would you like to have lunch with me? You could meet me at the office.'

She looked up eagerly. 'Yes,' she said, 'I would.'

She had never been to his office, never felt that she would be welcome there. She regarded the invitation as some kind of milestone in their marriage.

For that reason she dressed carefully for their lunch date, and was rewarded by a quick glow of appreciation in Shard's eyes when his secretary ushered her into his presence.

He had a sheet of paper before him, and a pen in his hand. 'Sit down,' he said. 'I just want to finish this.'

Instead of doing that, she walked over to the huge drawings pinned on to one wall. They showed a high-rise building and were obviously architect's plans.

Shard put down his pen and came to stand beside her, his arm hooking about her waist.

'Is this what you're working on now?' he asked.

'Our biggest project—the Dunfield Building,' he said.

'We've just begun the actual construction work.'

'What does all this mean?' she asked, pointing to a sheet of diagrams with notations on it.

'That's one of the working drawings,' he said, and explained to her some of the terms, his face alive and purposeful.

Then he laughed and said, 'Come on, I promised you lunch.' On the way out Elise was introduced to some of the staff, who looked at her curiously but in a friendly way; and she recognised one or two who had been at the party.

When they had finished their meal, Shard looked at his watch and said, 'I have to go down to the Dunfield site. Sorry to rush you, but you would insist on studying those drawings.'

'Can I come?' she asked. 'I'd like to see the real thing.'

'There's not much to see,' he said. 'And you're hardly dressed for scrambling round a construction site.'

Elise looked down at her empty coffee cup, fighting a sudden bleak hurt.

She felt his hand over hers, and he said, 'Come if you want to. If I'd meant, *no, you can't,* I'd have said it.'

She wasn't dressed for it, but she stood in her high heels and pretty dress, with Shard's jacket pulled about her shoulders against the brisk wind, and watched him, in overalls and a hard hat, scrambling about the iron scaffolding and walking confidently along the narrow boards it held, talking to the workmen and watching with keen eyes the working of the huge crane overhead as it swung long steel girders into place.

She was aware of the activity all about her, the noise of heavy machinery, the ringing of hammers on steel, but she concentrated on Shard's tall figure, his windruffled hair when for a moment he removed the hard hat and then resettled it firmly on his head, his white smile.

When he swung down and came across the rough ground to join her, she didn't smile, but her eyes were held by his all the way. He stopped before her and he, too, was unsmiling. Then he put his arm about her shoulders and turned her towards the car.

Through the varied noises of the construction and the muted hurly-burly of the nearby street, the wail of a distressed child came high and keening, and a small girl of about three or four wandered into view, knuckles to her eyes, and tripped on the ramp that crossed the dug-up pavement from the site to the road.

Instinctively, Elise ran forward, her skirt brushing the mud as she stooped to the little girl and placed her quickly on her feet, looking about for a parent as she did so.

None seemed to be in evidence, and as the child had skinned a knee and was now wailing more loudly than ever, Elise turned her attention to comforting her instead. To Shard, standing beside her, she said, 'Have you got a hanky, Shard? My bag is in the car.'

He produced one in silence and she used it to wipe the tear-streaked little face, and then the bloodied knee, talking all the while in a soothing voice.

'Where the hell is the child's mother?' Shard asked forcefully.

'Or father,' said Elise coolly. 'Shh, now, sweetie,' she added to the still sobbing child. 'We'll look after you until someone comes to find you. I'm sure they won't be long.'

'*Mummee!*' the child wailed in great distress.

'Was Mummy with you?' Elise queried gently, receiving a gulping nod in return. 'Well, I'm sure it won't be long before she comes along looking for you. Why don't you sit in the car with me, and let me put a plaster on this knee, while we wait for her?'

She received a doubtful look, but the sobs were lessening a little, and when she said, 'Would that be all right?' the little girl stared for a moment with watery blue eyes and then nodded again.

'I'll carry her,' said Shard. But when he stooped, the child shied away, throwing her chubby arms about Elise's neck and threatening to burst into renewed tears.

'I can manage,' Elise smiled, and picked up her burden to convey her the few steps to the car.

She sat with the door open, the child on her lap, while Shard found the first aid box and opened it. He tipped disinfectant on to cottonwool, but the little girl shied away when he made to apply it to the wound.

'What's your name?' Elise asked her gently.

'Debbie.'

'Well, Debbie, the nice man wants to fix the bleeding for you—he'll try not to hurt.'

Shard shot her a sardonic glance, and Debbie asked doubtfully, 'Is he your daddy?'

'He's my husband. That means that if I had a little girl like you, he would be her daddy. Does your daddy put a plaster on you when you get hurt?'

'Sometimes. Mostly Mummy does.'

Elise gave Shard a small nod, and kept talking while he cleaned the scraped skin and pressed a plaster over it. Debbie seemed uncertain about where she lived, but her full name was Debbie Marie Harris. 'When's my mummy coming?' she asked, her eyes filling with tears again.

Elise, looking in vain among the lunchtime shoppers hurrying by, said, 'I expect she won't be long. Do you know what she was wearing, Debbie?'

But Debbie didn't, and Shard, his voice edged with
something that Elise thought was impatience, said, 'I'll
go and look for a young woman with an anxious
look——' and got out of the car.

Elise got out a small notebook and pencil and when
Shard returned fifteen minutes later with an almost hys-
terically grateful young woman pushing another small
child in a pushchair, Debbie was happily watching as
she drew dogs, cats and rabbits and kept up a distract-
ing conversation.

'I only turned my back for a *minute*,' the mother exclaimed, guilt and embarrassment obviously vying with
gratitude. 'That was *naughty*, Debbie, you must stay
with Mummy.'

'There was a pussycat,' the child explained. 'But it ran
away.' The woman threw Elise a despairing glance, which
drew from her a smile of understanding. 'And,' Debbie
went on, 'I fell over and made a bleed, and the nice
daddy fixed it.'

'You've been very kind,' Mrs Harris said to both of
them.

Shard didn't look kind, he looked hard and aloof, and
anxious to get away. As he started the car, Elise answered Debbie's happy wave, glanced at him in puzzlement and asked, 'Are you late?'

'For what?'

'For—anything,' she said helplessly. 'You seemed in a
hurry.'

'Did *you* want to sit there all day being thanked?'

'No, of course not.'

But his impatience had shown itself before then. It
struck her that she had never seen Shard with a child
before. Perhaps he had, like many men, very little experience of children, and had reacted to an unusual
sense of inadequacy with irritation.

His attention concentrated on negotiating the darting lunchtime traffic, he looked remote and hard. Elise didn't blame Debbie for being a little nervous of him.

He still looked a little remote when he came in that evening, and she sensed a tension in him. As she served up the meal for them, he asked suddenly, 'Are you sure you don't want a paid household help?'

Surprised, she said, 'No. I like cooking and I don't mind housework—it isn't worth getting someone in for the little there is to do, anyway. There are only the two of us, and we don't entertain much.'

His look was keen but unreadable. 'You're working, after all——' he said.

Elise smiled. 'I've nearly finished the drawings for the textbook, and I don't know if any more work will be coming in.'

'It would if you looked for it.'

'Do you think I should? Do you want a career woman for a wife?'

'I want *you* for my wife,' he said quietly. 'Whatever you happen to be. Even——'

The flash of bitterness in his eyes was quickly hidden as he broke off, but she thought she knew what he had been going to say. *Even if she happened to be another man's widow.*

'I can't help what I am, Shard,' she said, deliberately hardening her voice to control the threat of its trembling. 'When you married me you knew——'

'Yes, I knew,' he interrupted harshly. 'You can be devastatingly frank at times, Elise. But I'm glad of that— at least I know just where I stand.'

'I can't hold a candle to you,' she said. 'You're the most brutally candid person I know—although lately you seem to be a little more——'

His eyes mocked her. 'Civilised? So you've noticed my efforts to reform.'

Nettled, she felt a faint rising of her old antagonism. 'My mother said marriage had mellowed you,' she informed him smugly, deliberately waving a red rag.

His narrowed eyes showed an appreciation of her mood. 'Didn't she give you credit for it?' he asked, the mockery still in his smile.

Almost defensively, she said, 'I've never asked you to change.'

'No.' Almost gently he added, 'But it pleases you, doesn't it?'

Elise wasn't sure about that. If anything, Shard's suave courtesy to her parents had made her a little uneasy. 'Do you want to please me?' she asked in a low voice.

'I want you to be happy.'

She searched his face and found it impossible to tell if he was absolutely sincere or still amusing himself.

She pushed away her plate and stood up to go to the kitchen for the dessert.

Later on, as she sat leafing through a magazine and Shard stood at the window of the lounge after a series of restless movements about the room, he suddenly turned to her and asked, 'Elise, would you like to adopt a child?'

'Would *you*?' she asked, staring at him. He had never indicated that he had wanted children, never given any hint that it mattered to him that she apparently couldn't have any.

But his quick movement as he came towards her was impatient. 'I asked what *you* want,' he said. 'If you want a child, we can do it.'

'For heaven's sake!' she exclaimed in sudden anger. 'You can't decide to adopt a child simply to satisfy my —my maternal instincts. A child has to be wanted—by both parents!'

'I didn't say I didn't want it. *Would* it satisfy your maternal instincts?'

'No! Oh—I don't know. That isn't the point.' She stood up, facing him. '*You* of all people should know,' she said, 'you can't just make a gift to me of a child, as though it was a—a fur coat or a watch! There are some things your money won't buy for me, Shard.'

He looked taut and angry. 'It isn't a question of money,' he said.

'No,' she admitted, turning away from him. 'It's more than that. It's this—compulsion of yours to give me everything I want. You saw me with that little girl to-day, and decided I might like one of my own—just as when I admire a painting or a piece of jewellery you get it for me. It doesn't matter if you happen to hate it yourself—and you never say. Suddenly you have no tastes, no opinions, no preferences, except a preference for pleasing me! I suppose I should be grateful and flattered —I'm not. I'm—I'm *suffocated*!'

He took a stride towards her and she evaded him and almost ran out of the room. She slammed the door of the bedroom and stood quivering in the middle of the floor, trying to calm herself. It was stupid to react like this. One got nowhere with emotional outbursts; she should have spoken calmly, reasoned with him.

The door opened and he came in, quietly closing it behind him. Without looking at him, she said in the calmest voice that she could muster, 'I'm sorry, Shard, I didn't mean to hurt you.'

He had been moving over the carpet towards her, but when she spoke he stopped short. He made some short, sharp exclamation under his breath, and then moved again, catching her shoulders in hard hands, as her startled eyes met his.

'Cut out the ladylike apologies,' he said, his mouth a

curve of sarcasm. 'You started to tell me what you really feel, in there.'

'I was angry———'

'Yes, you were. And interesting, until you ran away. It's what you always do, when a genuine emotion threatens to break through that iron-clad self-control of yours.'

'That isn't true!' she flashed, and saw the quick satisfaction in his eyes as his hands loosened.

'All right, forget that,' he said. 'Tell me why you feel suffocated.'

'I don't *know*! Except that you give me so much and ask for nothing.'

'I won't ask for what you can't give me. And what you do have to give, I've never had to ask for.'

Perplexed, she shook her head and queried, 'What are you talking about?'

'This,' he said, and reached for her again, pulling her fully into his arms.

She didn't respond at first to his kiss, standing rigid in his arms as his lips coaxed and then commanded. When his hands moved and touched her she gave a little shiver and made a small effort to escape. She still felt puzzled and resentful, and his answer was no answer, but a mind-bending, deliberately sensuous evasion.

He let her push him away a little, but only so that he could lift her and place her on the bed, and then silenced her fretful protest again with his mouth, and stilled her struggles with his hands, half coercive and half caressing, and the warm weight of his body against hers.

CHAPTER NINE

AFTER she had finished working on the textbook, Elise visited the office and the building site several more times, sometimes making sketches as the office block began to rise and take shape.

She also consulted quite often with Cole Finlay about the designs for their house. Shard seldom joined them, saying that Elise might please herself about the details.

Cole was a relaxing person, easy-going and with a quiet sense of humour. Elise discovered that he had once been married, had three children who now lived at the other end of the country with his wife and her second husband. 'I see them occasionally,' he said. 'It's what's known as an amicable arrangement. But it's odd seeing your kids only a couple of times a year. Every time, we have to get to know one another all over again.'

She thought he was lonely and a little sad, and often invited him for a meal, sometimes impromptu.

'Your wife took pity on me again,' he said to Shard one evening when Shard came home to find him once more ensconced in the lounge with a drink while Elise prepared the meal.

As Elise came out of the kitchen, Shard poured himself a drink, saying, 'You don't look a pitiable object to me, Cole.'

'Ah, but you're not a beautiful woman! Elise sees beneath the surface.'

Shard poured a glass of sherry and handed it to Elise, watching her face. 'Is beauty a necessary quality for that?' he asked.

Cole laughed. 'Maybe not, but it certainly makes it more enjoyable.'

'To be pitied? I can't imagine that being enjoyable under any circumstances.'

Elise said lightly, 'Cole's talking nonsense. I asked him to stay for dinner because I—we—enjoy his company. Besides, I want him to show you the latest plans for the house. You never have time during the day.'

'I'll get them,' said Cole, and putting down his glass left the room, adding, 'They're in the car. Won't be long.'

Shard leaned back in his chair, his gaze on Elise, going without haste from her neatly crossed ankles to her gleaming, swept-up hairstyle. '*Are* you sorry for him?' he asked.

'A little.'

'He's successful, healthy, reasonably well off——'

'And has a broken marriage and three children he scarcely ever sees. He misses them.'

Shard's eyebrows rise. 'So he's taken you into his confidence.'

'You didn't know?'

'I knew he was divorced.'

'I suppose men don't talk about these things much.'

'Not to me.'

Elise looked at him thoughtfully. 'No, not to you. You don't really seem the marrying kind at all, Shard. Sometimes I wonder why you——'

'But you know why,' he said. 'You wouldn't settle for less.' He stood up suddenly, his eyes gleaming but unreadable. 'And neither could I. I wanted you completely and for ever. You know that.'

The liquid in her glass danced a little. 'I wasn't sure,' she said. 'You seem to live from day to day. I didn't know if *for ever* was included in your calculations.'

Deliberately he said, 'I don't make vows unless I'm

going to keep them. There seems to be a lot about me that you don't know.'

'You're not easy to understand,' she said.

'Why? I thought my main fault in your eyes was being too direct.'

'Have I said that?'

'I certainly thought so. In actions as well as in words.'

She studied his face, wondering if he found her over-critical, and thinking that although he had been harsh about her character when they first met, he never criticised her now—except for that one time when he had bitterly accused her of marrying Peter to please everyone but herself . . . and him.

Then Cole came back, carrying a folder, and Shard moved away to speak to him as he began pulling out sheets of plans. Elise finished her drink and returned to the kitchen.

There were times when she felt that she had come close to fathoming some of the depths in Shard, but each time she would come up against something that baffled and bewildered her. Although he never lied and seemed to say just what he thought, she felt that three-quarters of him was deliberately hidden from her. It put a restraint on her own emotions and she was well aware that at times Shard looked at her with a sardonic, narrow smile when she was treating him to her coolest and most exquisite good manners. Occasionally she would look up to find him studying her with laughter in his eyes, and if she met them an unspoken message flashed across the space that separated them—a message that made her look away with burning cheeks, hoping that no one else, if they were in company, had seen. Because it was so blatant, and because she couldn't prevent her own eyes from signalling the answer that he wanted.

Because in the privacy of their bedroom she couldn't maintain that coolness, and he knew it. He knew the aloof courtesy was a façade that crumbled easily at the light touch of his fingers on her body, that he could change her cool poise to careless, clinging passion, and bring to her lips the incoherent sounds of love instead of polite platitudes.

But she too had her moments of triumph when for a short but endless space of time he lay in her arms and gave himself to her in the uncontrollable culmination of his passion. At those times it seemed that this was all that really mattered, this completeness in each other was the reality, and the hidden barriers she felt at other times were an illusion.

The calendar had suddenly become an important factor in her life. She was counting days, first with some surprise, then with hope and now with a barely suppressed excitement. She told herself she dared not hope, that it was too soon to even consult a doctor, that she mustn't count on the miracle. But the excitement kept welling up past the caution and the common sense with which she tried to contain it, and also past her doubt as to Shard's likely reaction.

Shard didn't seem a family man, but he would accept this—if it was true—for her sake. And in time he must, surely, love his child for its own sake?

But she would have to be sure before she mentioned it to Shard. It wasn't really a miracle, of course. The doctors hadn't said it was impossible, just unlikely.

Elise had no further commissions, but she had started on an ambitious project, a book of her own. It would be a picture book, with a simple text which she wrote herself, the story about a little boy whose father was a builder, and was building a home for himself, his wife and child. She used the sketches she had made on Cortland Construction sites, and adapted them to the story, where the father took the boy to see some of the building projects he was engaged in. And she used the knowledge that she picked up from Shard and Cole for the technical details of the planning and construction of the house.

She went out to the site of their own house one day and watched and asked questions as Cole took measurements and checked levels. She was standing watching the blue sea wash lazily into the beach below when a sudden wave of dizziness caught her, and she clutched at a nearby tree, leaning her clammy forehead against the rough trunk.

Cole's voice came to her dimly. 'Elise, what's the matter?'

Gratefully she leaned on his arm and let him take her back to the car.

'Get your head down,' he ordered. She obeyed and after a few minutes was able to sit up, gulping air.

'Sorry,' she gasped. 'I'm all right now. Thank you, Cole.'

'I'll take you home,' he said. 'You still look a bit rocky.'

'But you haven't finished——'

'Never mind. You need to lie down properly.'

Gratefully she sank back in the seat and let him take charge.

When they arrived he accompanied her into the flat, made her lie on the bed and insisted on making tea. He had even made fingers of crisp brown toast, she discovered, when he carried a tray into the bedroom, and handed her the cup of steaming liquid.

It made her feel better, and Cole said, 'Now you look more like yourself.'

'I feel it, too.'

'Have some toast. It'll help.'

She would have said she couldn't eat, but she took a finger of it to please him, and surprised herself by eating it all. 'You're right,' she said. 'You missed your vocation, Cole, you should have been a nurse.'

He grinned a little sadly. 'I've been through it before,' he said. 'Every time my wife was expecting she was like this for a few weeks.'

Elise flushed. 'I'm—not certain yet,' she said.

'I am,' he smiled. 'Some women get a certain glow about them when it happens. You're one of them. I've noticed it a couple of times in the last week or so. It's like a light going on inside you, that shows in your face. You're always beautiful, but lately I've seen you grow even more so. And I've envied Shard—now, more than ever.' He smiled. 'I'd better go—stay here, I know where the door is.'

She put out her hand, and he took it. 'You were wonderful——' she began, but he broke into her thanks with a smile.

'And you *are*!' he said, making her laugh and shake her head against the pillow.

He bent and dropped a kiss on her brow, and as he straightened and dropped her hand, Elise looked past him as a figure appeared in the doorway.

'Shard!'

Shard walked into the room, his face conveying no expression whatever, but a certain mask-like rigidity.

Cole said, 'I'm just leaving, Shard. Elise is a bit unwell.' He looked awkward and uneasy, trying too hard to be natural. 'We were out at the section,' he explained, 'so I brought her home and made a cup of tea when she started feeling seedy.'

Disturbed by Shard's continued silence, his eyes that were fixed with inflexible coldness on Cole's face, Elise swung off the bed and stood beside Cole.

'Cole's been awfully kind,' she said, her voice sounding to her own ears several notches higher than usual, almost unnatural. 'What are you doing home at this hour?'

The grey eyes swung to her face, stony and merciless. 'I have to go to Wellington for a few days,' he said. 'The plane leaves in an hour.'

He looked pointedly back to Cole, who shifted his feet and looked apologetically at Elise, then moved reluctantly to the door. 'I'll leave you to it, then,' he said lamely. And then, 'You should make her rest, Shard. Pregnant ladies need special care, you know.'

Elise saw him almost wince as Shard said, 'I can look after my wife, Cole.'

Cole smiled uncomfortably and Elise heard the outer door close behind him. She realised that they must have left it open, as he brought her inside, and so they hadn't heard Shard coming in.

Shard had turned his back on her and was opening the wardrobe, taking a small bag from it and throwing it on the bed, already taking shirts from hangers. Hadn't he heard what Cole had said?

She picked up one of the shirts and began folding it. Shard turned to the chest of drawers, pulled out socks and underwear and threw them into the bag.

'Don't you want to lie down?' he asked, stuffing a spare pair of shoes into a corner of the bag. There was sarcasm in his voice.

'I'm quite all right, now.'

He gave her a lightning look and said, 'Yes. You don't look sick.' He glanced at his watch and said, 'The taxi should be here by now.' He went to the bathroom, and came back with his shaver and toothbrush in his hands, put them into the leather toilet bag she had given him for Christmas, and tossed it into the case, shutting it. She didn't know anyone else, she thought, who could pack in five minutes.

She heard the sound of the taxi honking outside, and Shard picked up the bag.

She said, 'It's very sudden, isn't it?'

'Yes, they seem to have a crisis. I'll have to sort it out.'

'You'll be back on Friday?'

She might have imagined the small pause before he said, 'Yes.'

He was moving to the door, and the taxi driver must have got impatient, because the doorbell rang as Elise said, 'Shard——?'

He turned and looked at her.

She said, 'Did you hear what Cole said?'

His mouth was hard and his jaw set. 'About what?' he said.

'About—why I was feeling sick. I'm going to have a baby, Shard.'

'Oh, yes,' he said, as though it was an unimportant bit of information that had slipped his mind. 'Whose?'

For a moment he stood there, as she whitened and her breath sucked into her throat in sudden, tearing pain. Then, unbelievably, he turned on his heel and walked out.

For a long time Elise stood where he had left her, the echo of the slamming door still in her mind. She had an almost superstitious feeling that she mustn't move, because surely, *surely* Shard would come back and tell her he hadn't meant it. He wouldn't get on the plane and fly to Wellington without retracting that cruel and preposterous accusation.

After a while she sat down on the bed, grasping the slippery satin of the spread because she felt a dire need to hold on to something. But it didn't help. The one thing

that was clear in her mind, as she looked at the little bedside clock and saw that the hour was up and the plane
must be taking off, was that Shard of all people never
said anything that he didn't mean. He was never petty
and he didn't know how to pretend, and besides, what
reason could he have for pretending that he believed she
could have been unfaithful to him?

The only explanation was that jealousy had warped
his judgment. And yet—and now anger began mercifully
to mitigate the hurt—he had no reason to be jealous.
There *was* no reason, nothing except the fact that she
and Cole, both fully dressed, had been in the bedroom
when he came unexpectedly home in mid-afternoon. She
supposed that at first sight the situation might have
looked compromising, with Cole's farewell gesture in
mind—that quick, light brushing of his lips against her
forehead. But any reasonable man would have accepted
the true explanation, not made a vicious accusation
against a friend and the wife he had every reason to
trust.

A long time later, she began to feel a strange empti-
ness, and realised that she was hungry. Her mouth
smiled wryly as she got up and went through to the kitchen. Human nature was strange. She felt as though it
didn't matter if she never ate again, but a healthy body
wasn't concerned with the delicate feelings of the mind.
She remembered the same feeling after Peter's funeral,
when she had vaguely thought it was a part of her grief,
and Shard had come and forced her to realise that this
particular part of it was purely physical, after all.

Shard, who had come back into her life and made her
live again—made her love him as she had never loved
Peter. And who was responsible for the numbing, terrible
ache that she couldn't localise but that seemed to be in
her brain, her heart, her lungs, even in the hands that

clumsily buttered bread and broke eggs as she forced herself to make a meal she didn't want.

Because, as Cole had said, pregnant ladies must be looked after—she had another life to think of now, a very small, barely beginning human being that she scarcely dared believe in as yet, but that she felt was terribly precious and fragile.

She switched on the television after she had washed up, because the silence was so terrible, but she hardly understood what she watched. At ten, the announcer was babbling news about famine overseas, a plane crash somewhere, the collapse of a well-known finance business that a bearded commentator said had affected the financial situation of a number of other well-known firms as well as numerous small investors. The words went on, but Elise's ear was tuned to the sound of the telephone, that remained stubbornly silent.

Shard had been in Wellington for hours, now, within easy reach of a telephone, a quick toll-call to Auckland that would have taken a few minutes of his time. And there had been nothing.

She scarcely slept, and woke in the morning feeling unutterably depressed. As she came fully awake and conscious, the depression turned to sharp, searing pain.

She made breakfast to stave off a dizzying nausea, forcing herself to swallow toast and tea, and then went to the telephone and made an appointment to see the doctor later in the day. It was only sensible to confirm her condition, although she was sure there was no mistake. And besides, it gave the empty day some purpose.

She had barely put down the receiver when the bell pealed into the stillness. She snatched it up with a sudden lurch of hope that died abruptly when Cole's voice said, 'You must have been standing by the phone.'

'Yes,' she said, trying not to let her sick disappointment colour her voice, 'I was.'

'Been talking to Shard?' he asked, a little too casually.

'No. I haven't heard from him since he left yesterday.' Hastily she tacked on, 'I expect he has a lot to do.'

'Yes, I suppose so. It was pretty sudden, wasn't it?' He sounded sober.

'Very sudden,' she agreed, thinking of that lightning swift packing. 'We—didn't have much time to talk.' She realised she didn't even know the nature of the crisis that had summoned Shard to Wellington.

'When do you expect him back?' Cole asked.

'Friday. He said three days.'

'Well, if there's anything I can do, Elise——'

Keep well away, she thought. If Shard returned to find Cole hovering about her ...

'Nothing,' she said. 'I think I'll go to my parents until he comes back.'

'That's a good idea.' He sounded relieved. 'Well, keep in touch.'

'Yes,' she promised, 'I will.'

It hadn't been a comfortable conversation, with the memory of Shard's grim, accusing face between them. She wondered if they would ever regain the undemanding, pleasant friendship they had shared.

The telephone rang twice more, both times the callers asking for Shard. 'He's in Wellington,' she told them. 'I don't expect him back until Friday at the earliest.'

One of the callers laughed in what she thought was an odd way, and said, 'I see.'

She didn't know what it was he saw, and didn't care for his manner, so she bade him a frigid good morning and put down the receiver. She supposed they were business calls, which was unusual, but then it was unusual for Shard not to be in his office in Auckland during the day.

But she didn't want to stay here, her heart leaping into life each time the phone rang, only to plummet when the caller was not Shard. She lifted the receiver again, this time to dial her parents' number.

'I'd like to come and stay,' she told her mother. 'For a couple of nights, if that's okay. Shard's in Wellington——'

'Of course,' her mother said, with more warmth than usual in her voice. 'You must come to us, dear. What time——?'

'I'll come right over, if I may,' said Elise. Trying to smile, she added, 'I'm sick of my own company. But I have an appointment this afternoon.'

Once the decision was made, she felt better. She packed almost as quickly as Shard had, locking the door behind her with a sense of relief, grabbing the rolled newspaper from the delivery box as she passed, and dropping it on the floor of the car without glancing at it. She had troubles of her own enough this morning without reading about those of the rest of the world.

She was welcomed with a kiss and a warm hug that surprised her.

Her bag was put into her own room and her mother made tea. It was too soon after her breakfast, but Katherine's solicitude was so marked that she didn't like to refuse.

'Have you seen the paper this morning?' her mother asked.

'It's in the car, I haven't looked at it. Why?' asked Elise, trying to muster some interest. 'Is there anything new?'

'Well, at least the TV report didn't mention Cortland Construction by name. The paper printed it.'

Puzzled, and then afraid, Elise queried, 'What? What about Cortland Construction?'

'Well, what do you think?' said her mother, as though she must know all about it. She got up and took the paper out of the magazine rack across the room.

Unable to wait, Elise put down her cup with a little clatter and followed. 'Let me see,' she said, panic rising as she remembered Shard's grim haste yesterday, Cole's awkward offer of help, her mother's unusual tenderness —all taking on a new significance now.

She took the sheets from her mother's hands and her eyes dilated on the black front page headlines.

WIDESPREAD REPERCUSSIONS FROM FINANCIAL COLLAPSE

And below in bold type: *The sudden collapse of the giant and apparently ulta-safe finance and investment corporation Leed and Howell threatens many major business organisations with bankruptcy; these include Abingdon's Transport, Carroll and Mercer Ltd., Cortland Construction . . .*

The black type was blurred and dancing before her eyes. It seemed to run across the page and obscure the white paper, and there was a rushing hum in her ears. She felt cold as ice all over and her fingers could no longer hold the newspaper . . .

Her mother's voice seemed miles away, and she found herself lying on the sofa. She opened her eyes and the room tilted and then moved slowly into focus.

'Drink this,' Katherine said briskly, thrusting a small glass into her hand. She did, and it helped. Alcohol, but she didn't know what kind. It seeped into her cold limbs and warmed them a little.

'I'm sorry,' she said. 'How ridiculous—like a Victorian melodrama. That's the second time in two days.'

On a note of trepidation, Katherine asked, 'Are you pregnant?'

Elise managed a small smile. 'Yes, I think so. I'm going to the doctor this afternoon.'

'I'll come with you. But really, Elise, what a time to pick!'

Elise tried to laugh. 'I didn't really pick it,' she said. 'I never expected it to happen.'

'No. Well, it can't be helped. How does Shard feel about it?'

'I—I hardly had time to tell him before he flew to Wellington. He—I don't think he really took it in.'

'What on earth possessed you to tell him *then*?'

'I did mean to wait until the doctor confirmed it, but it sort of slipped out.'

Katherine looked as though she didn't quite comprehend that. In her experience things didn't 'slip out' unless they were meant to.

'You weren't trying to keep him with you, were you?' she asked with disapproval. 'A man must look after his business, Elise. It isn't a matter of putting it first, before you. He has to take care of it to enable him to take care of you. It would be childish to expect him to drop more important matters because you feel a little unwell and lonely.'

'It wasn't that,' Elise said. She was tempted to pour out the whole story, but the ready sympathy that Katherine had shown before was slowly evaporating, and confiding in her mother was a habit that had long since been discouraged. Failures and failings were in Katherine's mind something to be overcome by willpower and common sense, not grounds for an overdose of sympathy which only led to wallowing in one's problems instead of solving them. It was a philosophy that had distinct advantages but suffered a little from its lack of flexibility and a certain dearth of tenderness.

'You look better, now,' she said, and taking her cue, Elise sat up, swinging her legs to the floor.

'I'm all right,' she said bravely, although her temples still felt a little clammy and her hands tingled. Her mother despised weakness. 'I don't understand,' she said shakily, 'how Shard comes to be involved in this. The company is independent.'

'Your father explained it last night,' Katherine told her. 'Although I have to admit that I can't understand it completely either. He assumes I know the meaning of a lot of terms just because I've taken an intelligent interest in the business over the years, but I have to admit to *you* that half the time I'm saying, "Yes, dear, and what about the fixed share income?" I'm really thinking with half my mind of something else. Howard says all the companies are interrelated in some way through investments and loans, and that Shard is not to be blamed because the corporation was regarded as quite safe by most of the business community. The collapse has come as a tremendous shock—caused through over-confidence and over-investment, Howard said, and too much diversification into too many industries, whatever that means.'

'It means that Shard may lose everything that he's worked so hard for,' Elise said bitterly.

'Well, if the worst comes to the worst,' Katherine told her, 'Howard will make a job for Shard in the company. We decided on that last night.'

How Shard would hate that charity, Elise thought dispassionately. Aloud, she said, 'That's generous. Thank you.'

'Not at all. I won't have my daughter's husband going cap in hand to other people, asking for work.'

Elise winced. 'If he's bankrupt,' she said, 'We may be owing money. For a long time, perhaps.'

Unexpectedly, her mother patted her hand. 'It may not come to that. Howard says Shard's reputation is excellent, and he may well be able to pull the business out of all this, after all. I must admit that at first I was inclined to blame him, and blame ourselves for letting you marry him——'

'You couldn't have stopped me, Mother!'

'Well, be that as it may, I think your duty now is to stick by your husband and help him as much as you can until he's on his feet again.'

'Yes, of course,' said Elise, and looked curiously at her mother. 'You didn't think I would leave him, did you?'

'I'm sure you know better than that,' Katherine said austerely. 'But I do think that this marriage is perhaps a little—self-indulgent. You and Shard have very little in common, after all, and you must admit that he has accustomed you to having whatever you want. I should be disappointed if you faltered in your duty because times are less good than they were. I know that Shard attracted you a little, before you married Peter, but you very sensibly saw that *that* kind of attraction was superficial without a solid background, such as Peter could give you. Then when Shard asked you to marry him, you found you could have your cake and eat it, too, and I was pleased for you. But now you are going to find your marriage will be a severe test of your moral courage. I'm sure you'll stand up to it well, as you did to Peter's death.'

Weakly, Elise said, 'I—certainly hope so.' So her mother thought sexual attraction was all that bound her to Shard. How strange and rather frightening it was that someone who might have been closer than any other person on earth understood so little about her own daughter.

The doctor was congratulatory and a little concerned.

'In view of your history,' he told her, 'you must be extra careful. Eat sensibly and get plenty of rest. I'll give you some iron pills, too, which will help to stop these fainting turns, I hope. And I'll want to see you often. Nurse will give you an appointment.'

Her mother, who had insisted on accompanying her, was briskly solicitous, and Elise found that she rather enjoyed the unaccustomed pampering.

When her father was told the news that evening, she was touched at the warmth of the hug he gave her as he congratulated her. For a little while she pushed to the back of her mind the apprehension that flickered every time they mentioned Shard's name. It wasn't possible, she told herself, that he could really believe the baby might not be his. She refused to seriously think about it.

CHAPTER TEN

WHEN Shard came home Elise was waiting for him. She had been waiting for a long time, not knowing what time to expect him, and since she had not heard from him, unwilling to phone the airport and ask if they could tell her. If he had wanted her to know, she supposed that he would have contacted her. About the possibility of his not coming at all, she wouldn't let herself think. He had said he would return today. She waited.

It was late in the afternoon when she heard his key in the lock. She stood up from the chair where she had been trying to read, and listened as he entered the flat. There was a long pause, then she heard him put down his bag on the hall floor and begin slowly walking to the lounge.

He stood in the doorway and she saw that he was exhausted, his eyes dull with tiredness and his skin almost grey. He even seemed to sway a little as he stood there, and put up a hand to steady himself against the wooden frame of the door.

'You're here,' he said, his voice husky and toneless with weariness.

'Where else would I be?' she asked him.

He shook his head and his lips moved, but she wasn't sure if the movement was a smile.

She said, 'You're tired, Shard. Have you had any sleep?'

'Not much,' he answered dully. 'About——' he frowned as though trying to recall. 'About—six hours since I left, I think.'

He straightened and seemed to gather himself, his eyes

so intent on her face that Elise felt he was making a tremendous effort to concentrate and focus them on her instead of closing them. 'We have to talk,' he said slowly. 'I must talk to you.'

She moved towards him. 'Not now,' she said gently. 'You're dead on your feet, Shard. You must go to bed.'

He pushed his dark hair back off his forehead and said irritably, 'I'm all right. I want to talk to you.' He shook his head as if to clear it, and Elise said firmly,

'You're *not* all right, and I won't listen until you've had a sleep. You can't think straight, now, anyway. Anyone could see that.'

'Oh, God, you're right,' he admitted.

She took his arm, encouraging him to the bedroom, but he suddenly gripped her shoulders so fiercely that she winced, holding her in front of him so that she didn't know if he meant to push her away or pull her close to him. Behind the film of exhaustion in his eyes something else leaped and died.

'I don't need your help,' he said briefly. 'I'll manage.'

She watched him go into the bedroom, and ten minutes later followed him. He was lying on top of the bed, had taken off his shoes and nothing else. He was sleeping deeply.

She eased off his tie and undid two buttons of his shirt, but she couldn't move his dead weight to remove his jacket. She got a spare blanket and covered him with it. He didn't stir, his face relaxed and younger in sleep, the firm line of his mouth softened and the pallor of exhaustion now receding.

Elise picked up his bag from the hallway and moved quietly about, unpacking and putting away his things, taking the soiled clothes to the small laundry off the kitchen. It would have taken a cataclysm to waken him, she thought. She took the phone off the hook all the same. There had been several enquiries for him today, and she knew now that the callers were probably from the news media. So far Shard had made no statements, and she was sure he wasn't eager to talk to any reporters.

She inspected the contents of the freezer and made a casserole, a hearty savoury dish that could be heated and eaten whenever he decided to wake.

When he did, it was dark, and she was lying beside him. She had showered and put on a flimsy belted robe, and turned on the bedside lamp without disturbing him, and tried to read.

She knew he was waking when his breathing changed, and when his eyed opened and focused on her she was watching him.

But no sooner had the light of full consciousness returned to them than he shuttered his eyes and put his hand across them and then sat up. He looked at the clock and made some exclamation, and swung off the bed.

'I rang the office,' Elise told him, 'and told them you were here, but not to tell the reporters. They said no messages that can't wait until tomorrow.'

'Thank you,' he said. 'I need a shower.'

While he was in the bathroom she reheated the casserole and cut some thick slices off a French loaf to go with it.

Shard came into the kitchen with his hair still damp from the shower, doing up the belt of his towelling robe. 'You're not cooking at this time of night——?' he queried. 'I don't need anything.'

'I cooked it hours ago,' she said. 'And you do. It's all ready, so eat it.'

'Oh, for God's sake,' he sighed wearily. 'Must you go on playing the perfect wife?'

Her hand tightened on the spoon she was placing in the steaming casserole. Without a tremor she said, 'Perhaps we could discuss that later. I've just reheated this. Please don't let it get cold again.'

He bit back something he had been going to say, and sat down while she waited on him. He ate a good helping of the casserole, refused ice cream and fruit, and drank two cups of coffee while she sat opposite and drank one.

Then he pushed away his cup and said, 'You know, of course, what's happened.'

'Yes. Not the finer details, but in general terms. Is it very bad? How much have you lost?'

'I'm not sure yet just how bad. I'm trying to salvage what I can. But I stand to lose everything I have.'

'Oh, Shard, I'm so sorry!'

She saw him clench his fists on the table, and he said: 'You can have a divorce any time you like.'

At first Elise didn't believe she had heard aright. And then, when she knew that she had, she found herself shaking with a pure white flame of anger. She pushed back her chair, moved to leave him and found herself clinging for support to the chairback. She wished she had the strength to pick it up and throw it at him. Her voice clipped and brittle, she snapped, 'Thank you! I suppose that's the only thing you have left now to give me.'

His shoulders tensed. 'Yes,' he agreed, 'that's probably right.'

'Do you really think that's what I want?' she asked. 'Do you?'

He suddenly pushed back his chair and rose to face her. 'You wouldn't have married me if I hadn't had money,' he said flatly. He stopped her quick protest with a slashing, savage gesture of his hand. 'It's true!' he said. 'You were frank about it at the time, don't start being squeamish now, for God's sake! You wanted me, yes, but you found that no hardship to resist as long as you thought

I had no prospects of success and a good income. Don't think I'm complaining, Elise. I was grateful for your honesty—at least it left me no illusions to be shattered. And for your passion, it was all I'd hoped for. I think I carried out my part in the bargain fairly well, but now I'm no longer in a position to do that. So I won't hold you to your part.'

For a moment it seemed wildly funny that Katherine and Shard had apparently both assessed her character and her motives in the same way, but Elise recognised the hysterical desire to laugh and bit her tongue to stop it. She knew the doubt that had kept her from acknowledging and giving into her feelings for Shard had been nothing to do with his money or his success. Yet Shard was talking of her 'frankness' as though she had admitted to him that it was.

'I don't understand you——' she began helplessly.

'No,' he said. 'You never did.'

He turned away from her and left the room. Elise moved her fingers from the chairback and discovered that they ached, her hold on it had been so tight. Automatically she stacked the dishes in the sink, then braced herself to go into the bedroom.

Shard was dressed in trousers and a shirt that he was just buttoning up.

'Are you going out?' she asked.

'To the office. I won't sleep any more tonight, anyway, and there are things to be cleared up there, too.'

'Will it make a difference?' she asked. 'If you go tonight instead of tomorrow morning, will it help to save the business?'

'No. It won't save the business.'

'Then,' she said, 'I think I have the right to ask you not to go.'

He was half turned from her, his fingers on a button of

his shirt. She saw him tense, and then he turned to look at her, and in the dim light from the bedlamp his eyes seemed to be suffering. His hands fell away from the button and for a moment the palms turned to her almost in a supplicating gesture. Then he shrugged and said, 'If you insist.'

She said, 'You've accused me more than once of running away from things. I thought *you* were above that.'

'I wasn't running away. I just don't see any point in going over the ashes.'

'I don't *want* a divorce!' she told him fiercely. 'I've become used to you deciding what I want and then giving it to me, but this time your—generosity—is out of hand, not to say ludicrous! I won't accept a divorce.'

She moved, coming towards him, into the circle of the lamplight. She felt cold and sick and her knees trembled.

Shard drew in a quick, harsh breath and moved suddenly to put his hand under her elbow, and then his fingers gripped her arm.

'For God's sake lie down,' he said. 'You're ill.'

'Not really.' But she sank thankfully down on the bed as he stripped off the covers and helped her into it. Her head felt heavy on the pillow and she closed her eyes thankfully for a moment.

When she opened them, Shard was standing looking down at her, his mouth a harsh line and his eyes dark and glittery. 'Please don't look like that,' she whispered, reminded of his expression when he had come in and found her here with Cole. 'You're wrong about me, Shard. So terribly wrong——'

She felt the tears coming and turned her head away, desperately closing her eyes to stop them.

She felt his hand grip hers, and fingers brushing the tumbled hair from her cheeks. She gasped, trying to stifle a sob, and gritting her teeth, managed a few words. 'You've got to listen———'

'Not now,' he said. 'We can talk in the morning. You made *me* sleep, now it's your turn.'

She felt him withdrawing his hand from hers, and she clutched. 'Don't go away!' she begged in panic.

'Shh!' he said, and she thought that his lips brushed against her fingers. 'I'm not going anywhere. Go to sleep.'

She woke to the sound of voices, floating intermittently from the lounge. She heard her mother's clipped, clear tones, and her father's deeper, forceful and persuasive voice. Then Shard sounding curt and controlled. The words were inaudible, but she had a picture of Shard trying to hold on to his temper in the face of her father's well-meant offers of help, and her mother's determined and deadly charity.

The clock stood at almost ten, and brilliant light seeped into the room around the edges of the drawn blind. Elise sat up suddenly and had to lie back for a moment to fight a wave of dizziness. The next time she did it cautiously, gradually getting her feet to the floor, and making gingerly for the bathroom.

When she had dressed and pulled a brush quickly over her hair, she pulled the bedroom door to behind her and heard the sudden lull in the sounds from the lounge as she walked towards it.

Shard was standing, his eyes darkly watchful as she appeared in the doorway. Howard was sitting in one of the armchairs, leaning forward as though trying hard to make some point to Shard, his brow creased with effort. And Katherine looked poised and pretty and anxious on the sofa.

'Elise dear,' she said, 'come and sit down. Howard had business to discuss with Shard, and I came to see how you were this morning, but Shard said you were sleeping. I'm glad you're taking the doctor's advice seriously.' As Elise obeyed, she turned to Shard. 'You must take very special care of her now, you know, Shard.'

'Yes,' he said, 'I've been told that.' His voice was even, but as his eyes rested on Elise they held a savage mockery, and her heart plunged in sudden fear.

'Will you promise to think about it, at least?' Howard was saying to Shard.

Formally Shard answered, 'I'll think about it. And thanks for the offer.'

He looked taut and fed up, and even as Elise turned to tell her mother that yes, she had slept very well, and she had started taking the iron pills, she felt a tremor of apprehension.

'I'll make some tea,' she said, getting up.

'Not for me,' said Howard. 'I've got to get back to the office.'

'I've stayed away from mine long enough, too,' Shard said. 'Why don't you stay for lunch with Elise, Katherine, and keep her company.'

Howard said heartily. 'Good idea—we'll leave the girls to gossip, shall we?'

Shard avoided Elise's looks of slightly despairing appeal, and turned with Howard to the door. Three minutes later they were both gone, and Katherine said, 'You know, I could *do* with a cup of tea. Your husband is really very difficult to help.' Her tone was light and almost humorous, but Elise heard the exasperation behind it.

'Yes,' she said, 'he can be very—determined.'

She found the next few hours wearing, trying to concentrate on her mother's sweet-sour comments on mutual acquaintances and the accounts of various social and charitable functions she had attended recently, inter-

spersed with advice on managing a husband, pregnancy
and children. As she left, Katherine said, 'You know,
I'm quite looking forward to being a grandmother. Now
don't disappoint me this time, will you, dear? Look after
yourself.'

'Yes, I will,' Elise promised mechanically.

'Have a rest, now—promise me!'

'Yes.'

Elise closed the door and leaned against it tiredly.
Her body felt weary and aching, but her brain was over-
active. She kept thinking of how Shard had looked at her
this morning without tenderness or a vestige of understanding. He had promised that this morning they would
talk, but instead he had left the flat as soon as he
decently could. Almost as though he couldn't bear to be
in the same room with her.

The telephone shrilled, making her jump. She looked
at it with hatred. It never carried good news these days.
It was never Shard.

Tempted to let it ring, she thought perhaps *this*
time . . .

But it was Cole, asking for Shard.

'He's at the office,' Elise told him wearily.

'Wrong,' he said. 'I tried there and they said he'd gone
out but they didn't know where. They suggested I try
his home.'

'I don't know where he is.'

A pause. 'Are you all right, Elise?'

'I'm fine.'

'No more dizzy spells?'

'One or two, but the doctor's given me a course of
iron.'

'That's the ticket. You know, when Shard came in the
other day, for a fantastic moment I thought he'd got
the wrong idea—about you and me. Of course later I

realised that he'd just had a nasty shock, about the finance business, which accounted for his odd expression. How is he, now?'

'Coping,' she said. 'Very well.'

'He would, of course. Pleased about the baby, is he?'

'Delighted,' she said.

He didn't notice the irony in her voice. 'Well, there's a silver lining,' he said. 'Tell him I was after him, would you?'

'Yes, I will.'

'And don't forget what I said about helping out if you need it. I meant it.'

'Thank you. Goodbye, Cole.'

She lay on her bed and tried closing her eyes against the hot burning sensation behind them, but couldn't sleep. She wondered where Shard was. Not on his way to her, she was sure.

When he did come in, it was later than usual, and she was in the kitchen, surrounded by a culinary aroma of herbs and wine and sour cream. She had chosen to cook a complicated and time-consuming meal to occupy her mind, and she had laid the table with care and precision, rejecting candles but making sure the cutlery was rubbed to a satiny sheen and the glasses sparkled on a beautifully ironed linen cloth.

Shard stopped in the doorway of the kitchen and she saw that his clothes were mud-splattered and his hair damp. Her hands were full with a pot of hot vegetables she was about to drain, and he said, 'Can it wait while I get cleaned up?'

'Yes, of course,' she said, and turned to place the pot in the sink. When she glanced up again, he had gone.

When he sat down, in open-necked dark shirt and casual fitting pants, he looked sardonically at the table and the steaming dishes and asked, 'Should I have dressed for dinner?'

She didn't answer, choosing to ignore the jibe. 'Where have you been this afternoon?' she asked. 'You weren't in the office.'

'Did you check up on me, my sweet wife?'

He was being deliberately unpleasant, and she saw no reason why she should let him get away with it. She said, 'I'm sure if there was anything I should check up on, you'd have covered your tracks very adequately.'

'I went to the Dunfield site,' he said abruptly.

She looked up. 'Are they still working on it?'

'No. The sub-contractors downed tools as soon as they thought there was a doubt about their getting paid.'

Elise remembered the way he had looked the first time she had seen the site, with the breeze blowing in his hair and his face raised to watch the swinging of the crane while below the workmen were busy and purposeful, drilling, hammering, digging, beginning the months of effort that would end in the handsome, ambitious structure pictured in the drawings on his office wall. Today he had been down there again, walking alone on the deserted duckboards and perhaps clambering up the scaffolding again where the skeleton of the building had begun to assume its future shape, the promise of permanence and solidity.

'What will happen?' she asked.

'It will go ahead. I saw Dunfield himself today.'

'That's good—isn't it?'

'Yes, that's good. But it doesn't get us out of the wood.'

'We'll manage,' she said. 'It will come right, Shard, I know it.'

He leaned back in his chair and looked at her, his eyes opaque, but his voice unmistakably jeering. 'Spoken like a loyal little wife,' he drawled.

Her voice hard, she said. 'That's what I am.'

'Yes, of course. And I should be grateful, shouldn't I? I've never been one to cry for the moon, after all.'

'No,' she said. 'If you wanted it you'd get up there and pull it down.'

'And if I did,' he said mockingly, 'maybe I'd find it was made of green cheese, after all.'

'How disappointing.' Determinedly she forked into her potatoes as though unaware what he meant. She was not giving him the satisfaction of knowing how much he hurt her.

She hardly expected to be complimented on her cooking, but when he had finished, Shard said, 'That was quite delicious. The way to a man's heart——'

The sting in the tail, she thought bitterly. 'It isn't like you to talk in clichés, Shard.'

'Maybe it's catching. You seem to think in them.'

'Is that remark supposed to mean something?' she enquired coldly. 'Or are you just being poisonous for the pleasure of it?'

He put down the wineglass he had been holding in his strong fingers and said, 'It's no pleasure. I assume that all this'—he indicated the table with its exquisitely careful setting now somewhat disarrayed—'is a softening-up process designed to smooth the way for that discussion we're supposed to have. Isn't it?'

'Actually,' she said, 'it was simply to give myself something to do while I waited. You did promise to talk this morning.'

'By the time I'd talked to your parents, I'd had about enough talking. Do you really think it's necessary?'

'You thought so, yourself, last night.'

'Did I? Last night seems aeons ago.'

Elise stood up. 'I'll bring coffee into the lounge. 'No, please don't help. I won't be long.'

Shard looked at her and shrugged and went into the other room. She washed the dishes quickly while the coffee brewed and took the two cups into the lounge. She felt nervous and keyed up, and Shard looked as though he was deliberately not giving anything away, his movements economical and controlled, his face hard, the grey eyes almost expressionless.

Elise sat herself on the sofa and he took a chair, and her throat ached for the many evenings they had shared the sofa, with his fingers threading through the softness of her hair against his shoulder.

He drank his coffee in silence and put the cup down. It seemed he wasn't going to help her at all. He looked up at her and waited with a studied politeness that was close to insult.

Her fingers tightening about her empty cup, she plunged straight in with the thing that was most stingingly in her mind, creating the deepest hurt and anger.

'When you left—for Wellington,' she began, 'the last thing you said to me . . . it was insulting and unfounded. This baby is yours, Shard. It's quite impossible that it could be anyone else's—and I resent very much the suggestion you—you seemed to be making about Cole and me.'

His expression didn't change. 'All right,' he said, 'I accept that—and apologise.'

The effect was as though he had shrugged and apologised for some minor mistake or social slip. She looked at him incredulously and her lips parted in a silent protest. She was filled with confused anger. Finally she managed, 'Is that all you have to say?'

'What else would you like me to say? I'm very sorry —I was wrong and stupid and I won't do it again? Is that enough?'

'Yes,' she said, 'it's enough.' Knowing that it wasn't,

that nothing would ever be enough but it was useless to
ask for more.

'Was there something else?' he asked.

'Yes,' she said. 'Did you offer me a divorce because
you thought that I wanted to marry someone else?'

'No.'

'Then why?'

'Because I would rather we made a clean break now
than see you gradually getting tired of expending your
wifely devotion on a man who can no longer give you
what you want.'

Her voice shook as she said, 'I don't give a *damn* for
what you can give me. And I want no break, clean or
otherwise, now or ever. I didn't marry you for your
money or your success, whatever you think—you said
I was frank with you, but I honestly don't know what
you were talking about ...'

Slowly he said, 'Don't you remember? The night you
gave in and agreed to marry me—you'd been fighting
all the way until then. And then you suddenly went
sweet and willing, and when I remarked on it you said
it was because you'd just found out what I'd assumed
you knew all along. "*You never told me you were Cortland Construction*" was what you said.'

'But, Shard——' she protested, 'it wasn't an answer! I
didn't mean it like that!'

He stood up, looking down at her distressed eyes as
they lifted to his face. 'It was an answer,' he said, 'how-
ever you meant it. It certainly marked the end of your
resistance.'

'Yes, but—it *wasn't* that!'

She stood up, touched his arm in pleading, about to
blurt out her uncertainty of six years ago, her distrust
of her own judgment, the apparent confirmation of her
fears when Shard had taken money from her grandfather

and disappeared to Australia. Then it struck her that he might be just as savage about her unfounded suspicions as he was about her seemingly mercenary motives for marrying him.

She hesitated, her thoughts racing, then said, 'Shard, I want to explain——'

He took her hand and moved it from his arm as though it was a piece of fluff or an importunate insect. 'Oh, no!' he said. 'At least spare me that.' He sounded weary and cynical and she knew that no matter what she said he wasn't going to believe her.

He was looking at her almost dispassionately. Her hands had fallen slackly to her sides and her shadowed eyes were dry, although there was a burning sensation behind them. His eyes rested indifferently on her still slim waist, the little shadow in the deep neckline of her dress, the soft hair swept up above her nape into a chignon.

'Are you sure you don't want that divorce?' he asked her.

'Yes, I'm sure!' she said with an effort. 'For heaven's sake, don't you realise—I'm going to have your baby!'

'I see. Yes, I suppose the nasty-minded might find something to think about in a divorce under the circumstances. What with that, and the danger of being accused of leaving me because I'm threatened with receivership, you don't really have much choice, do you?'

'I don't know *anyone* with as nasty a mind as *yours*,' she snapped. 'My decision has nothing to do with either of those reasons. The thought of leaving you never even crossed my mind.'

'Just let's be clear on one thing,' he said coldly. 'I haven't asked you to sacrifice yourself on the altar of your duty to me, and I won't help you to do it. And the last thing I want is your pity. If you stay with me it's because you want to for whatever reasons you care to give yourself. So don't expect any gratitude from me.'

Through quivering lips she said, 'No. No, I won't.'

She pushed past him and left the room. The flat suddenly seemed too small, and she ran a bath and spent a long time just sitting on the porcelain edge and pleating the folds of her dress with her fingers, until the water was cooling and she had to add more hot before she undressed and got into it. The bathroom was the only place where she could lock the door—and lock Shard out.

CHAPTER ELEVEN

ELISE supposed the nightmare must end some time. She seemed to be going through the motions of living although her heart had died within her.

Shard was bringing home paperwork now, and working far into the night, although he always ensured that she went to bed early. In that sort of thing he was punctilious, never letting her carry anything heavy, always adamant on doing the dishes, insisting that she rest. If he was going to be late he invariably telephoned to let her know. But he never addressed a personal word to her; they might have been total strangers who happened to share a home and a bed by reason of some freak of circumstance. Even when he found her hanging over the basin in the bathroom one morning, pale and gasping, there was something impersonal in his touch as he guided her back to bed and made her stay there while he made toast and weak tea for her. And every morning after that he made it before she got up, forbidding her to move before she had had it.

Once or twice Elise tried to resist his distant care, and he turned a brief, blazing glance on her and said with an almost vicious undertone, 'Just stay there!'

And she did. Because she didn't want that to happen too often. Sometimes she thought anything would be an improvement on the remote impersonal consideration with which he usually treated her now, but the shock of being snarled at changed her mind.

She had forgotten to give him Cole's message, but Cole must have caught up with him at some time, because one day he said, 'Cole was asking after you.'

A little cautiously she said, 'That's nice of him.' Something that had been part of the misery surfaced in her and she said, 'We can't have the house now, can we?'

She thought Shard wasn't going to answer. Then he said, 'Not for a while, anyway.'

The hollow ache inside grew. 'What about the land?' she asked. 'Will we have to sell it?'

His mouth went grim. 'Maybe.'

Elise sat still, remembering the shushing of the wind in the trees along the slight slope to the cliff, the blue water that was gentle between them, the singing of the cicadas in the summer and the calling of the bush birds that inhabited their little piece of unspoilt nature. She had imagined how they would sit on the sheltered terrace in the summer and listen to the birds and watch the leaves lifting in a sea breeze and the tiny blue-grey butterflies drifting across the lawn. There wouldn't have been much lawn, because they wanted to keep the trees that were there undisturbed, but there was enough of a clearing for a patch of grass and some plants, maybe a hibiscus or two and some azaleas near the edge of the patch of bush, and a rosebed.

It wasn't really much like the place where they had spent their honeymoon, that had been much wilder and rougher and more remote, with heavy breakers pounding along the sands and gulls screaming defiance at the winds that pushed them inland from the sea, and rocky crags at each end of the beach with battered ngaio and pohu-tukawa clawing the steep edges of the cliffs. But somehow when she went there she always felt an echo of the passionate, lovely days and nights that she and Shard had spent on a wilder shore when it seemed that nothing existed but the two of them and the delight that they found in being together after the long, long waiting . . .

Usually when Shard came to bed she was sleeping. If she woke when she heard him she would pretend to sleep anyway. Because now he never reached out his arms for her, never turned her to nestle into him, never stroked her hair or ran his fingers lightly over her body in invitation, or made sweet demands with his lips on her shoulder or nape.

But that night she woke fully and suddenly as he came into the room. He moved quietly and she lay still, pretending to sleep, until he lifted the covers and slid in beside her, but two feet away. It was always like that, now. She had been dreaming, and fragments of the dream returned as she listened to his breathing in the warm darkness. Shard laughing as they clambered over the rocks together as they had when they were first married, and still laughing as she slipped and fell into the surging water and was carried away from him screaming ...

Perhaps it was the horror of the dream that had woken her. She remembered it now in vivid, terrifying detail.

She moved restlessly, and knew that Shard had shifted his position too. She turned her head and in the darkness his eyes gleamed, open but unfathomable.

Tentatively she said, 'Shard?'

'What is it?' Perhaps it was the dark that made him sound more human than he usually did.

She moved nearer to him. 'I had a nightmare,' she whispered. Her hand reached out to touch his arm. 'Please hold me.'

He hesitated for only a moment, then his arms closed about her with great care, as though she was made of glass, and she put her cheek down on his chest and clung.

His breathing was deep and even as though he was asleep or nearly so, but when she moved her hand and it slipped inside the open edge of his pyjama top, it suddenly checked for an instant, and she knew he wasn't.

She hadn't intended anything but what she had said, to be held close to him for a little while until the beastliness of the dream receded. But now she wondered ... wondered if the closeness they had always found in lovemaking would still be there in spite of the bitter estrangement that existed, and if it was, surely it would help to break down the impenetrable barriers that Shard seemed to erect. She might be able to reach him in this one way, if no other ...

She moved her head again, deliberately stroking now, touching him with her fingers, in remembered ways, until he moved and his hard hand grasped her wrist. And his voice in her hair said, 'What do you want, Elise?'

Against the pounding of his heart, she said, 'You know what I want.'

His hands dragged at her hair, and he turned so that she was pinned against the pillow with his thumbs hard against her cheekbones and his fingers still in her tangled hair. His eyes gleamed and his breath was on her lips. 'Tell me,' he commanded, his voice low.

'Please, Shard——' she whispered. Her body moved a little against the hardness of his in remembered longing.

'Tell me what you want,' he said again, not moving.

'I want you—I want you to make love to me ...'

For a long moment he remained still, looking down at the white blur of her face, and she was suddenly afraid, afraid that he had dragged the words from her as a cruel joke, that he was going to reject her.

Then his head came slowly down and she felt his warm mouth claiming hers.

At first she was a little tense, but as he parted her lips with his and stroked her body with his hands she relaxed completely as the warmth of desire coursed gently through her. She knew that he had found the small changes in her body, his fingers lingering exploringly on the new firmness of her breasts, the slight roundness below her waist. And for a moment she was frightened again. But his kiss deepened as his hand lay on her stomach, until the unleashed passion of it hurt her lips and she whispered a protest.

He lifted his mouth and his hand moved again. The blind shifted in a little breeze from the window, and she saw his face with light shafting across it from the street-lamp outside. His mouth was smiling.

'Is this what you want?' he asked her, his voice demanding an answer.

'Yes,' she whispered. 'Yes—oh, please yes, Shard——'

He made love to her in ways that he knew she liked best, that sent her mindless and dizzy with delight, and each time he shifted their positions or touched her in a new way, he would pause, making her tell him what she wanted, making her put it into words, whispering her need to him.

And when finally he took her to the pinnacle of pleasure where no words were possible, she heard his soft laughter against her ear, and as her lips parted and her head fell back in ecstasy, she saw him lift his head, and in the light from the window his face was the face of her dream ...

The sound that tore out of her throat began as a cry of love, and ended as a scream of horror.

Shard's arms were a prison, and as his body shuddered against her she clawed at his shoulders, clenched her fists and pushed against him in frantic efforts at escape. As his hold loosened she tore his hands from her and her body, that had been pliant and welcoming moments ago, writhed in a frenzy of rejection.

As he lifted himself away the tears ran on to her pillow, and her voice was saying, 'No—no, no, no——'

as though she couldn't stop.

'What is it?' he demanded roughly. He took her shoulders in his hands, trying to see her face. 'Did I hurt you——? The baby?'

She shook her head, tried to pull away from him. 'No—*don't touch me*!' Her hands beat frantically at his arms and face, her breath coming out in sobbing gasps of fear and hysteria. And Shard lifted one hand and slapped her.

Her breath stopped and she went rigid. Then Shard's arms were about her, her tear-washed face against his bare shoulder, and his voice was raggedly against her hair, 'Oh, God! My darling, don't—please don't cry. I didn't want to hurt you—it's like tearing out my own heart——'

She couldn't speak, but she moved her cheek against his palm and felt his hand grip her shoulder as his lips touched her temple.

The tears gradually lessened, and she lay tiredly against him, her eyes closed. Shard eased her on to the pillow and left her, returning with a cloth wrung out in lukewarm water, and he sponged her face and body gently while she lay there, then eased her nightgown on and pulled up the covers. She felt his lips on her temple before she went to sleep.

She opened her eyes to dimmed sunshine and found fingers of cold toast and a cup of lukewarm tea on her bedside table. The place was quiet, and she felt a quick throb of disappointment. Shard must have left about half an hour ago, hoping she would wake in time to drink the tea before it cooled.

She tasted it and made a wry face, laughed a little for no reason at all, and stretched like a contented cat, full of well-being.

She ate some of the toast before getting up and taking a long warm shower and changing into slacks and a loose top. The slacks zipped up, but she couldn't fasten the button on the waistband. She smiled and patted her waist, then picked up the tray by the bed to take it to the kitchen.

She worked for a while on the sketches for her book, the little boy and his father now coming more easily than they had for weeks. The boy was a strong, wiry little boy with black curls and a serious expression, but she drew him laughing now, with his head back and his hands spread joyously, his feet planted apart on the rubble of a building site. And she drew the father with a smiling tenderness in his face as he looked at the boy.

For minutes at a time she was absorbed in her work, but as the morning wore on she found herself listening for the sound of the telephone. Tiny doubts began to infiltrate into the happy confidence with which she had woken.

Why had Shard gone without waking her? Was it consideration, or had he preferred not to face her in the light of day? He had made love to her, but he had made it some form of vengeance, and she had imagined it all wiped out by one endearment, a few words of remorse uttered in a moment of stress, and an act of kindness.

Was that enough to change everything? Perhaps Shard already regretted the momentary softening, and would return to her as cold and as cruelly distant as before.

She closed her eyes and her fingers tightened on the pencil in her hand, snapping the lead. It didn't bear thinking of.

She opened her eyes and saw the breaking of the pencil had scored a tiny black gash across the face of the man she was drawing, and her fingers shook as she carefully erased it.

If she could speak to him, his voice might tell her ...

She went to the phone and dialled the office, but his secretary said he was out and not expected back for some time.

'Do you know where he is?' Elise asked, her hand gripping the receiver in a dampened palm.

'He's meeting with a representative of Dunfield's and a bank manager, Mrs Cortland. I don't think he'd like to be disturbed, but if it's urgent I can try to reach him with a message——?'

'No—no, thank you,' said Elise. 'It isn't urgent.' *I just wanted to hear his voice* ...

'Would you like to leave a message for when he comes back, then?'

'No,' she said. 'No message.'

She went back to her table and spread out the drawings she had done, but the urge to add to them had dissipated. Leaving them, she wandered restlessly about, then came to a sudden decision, scooped the keys of her car off their hook, grabbed her purse and left. The car was another thing that might have to go, she supposed. It wasn't yet clear to her just how bad Shard's financial situation was.

She drove to the section, parking the car on the grass where the house had been going to stand, and sat looking out over the harbour. A rata was just coming into red bloom near the cliff's edge, and two fantails hopped about in its branches, restlessly perching and fluttering. She got out and approached softly for a closer look, but when she got near they flew off in a whirr of green-grey feathers.

She stood at the edge of the slope, and watched the cream-edged waves tentatively lapping at the strip of white sand below. And for the first time she noticed that someone had cut rough footholds into the face of the cliff, and in one place the protruding roots of the tenacious trees that clung to it made a series of natural steps.

The cliff was not very high or very steep, and the tiny bay looked very inviting. There were plenty of hand-holds among the trees and bushes that grew down the face. There was not much difficulty and very little danger in climbing down to the bottom.

She took it slowly and only became a little careless at the end, within a few feet of the sand. Her foot slipped a little and hooked under a curved root as she turned to make the last step, and as she leaped it caught and twisted with a jarring, wrenching pain in her ankle before her weight freed it.

She landed softly on the sand, unhurt otherwise, but very frightened for a few minutes while she lay there with her hand pressed to her stomach and her heart thumping.

She moved her foot, and her ankle throbbed pain-fully. She tried to rub it and winced, attempted to stand and thought better of it. The pain was too much.

After a while she half-crawled to the water's edge and lowered her throbbing limb into the blessed coolness. It was soothing, but when she tried her weight again the ankle was just as sore.

At one end of the little strip of sand the water reached a tumble of rocks, and she knew she could not negotiate them. At the other end there were overhanging trees, and when she dragged herself along to peer through the leaves she could see that further along the sand disappeared and the water washed against a sheer cliff. So there was no escape that way.

Perhaps if she rested for a while the ankle would heal itself at least sufficiently to allow her to climb back up the cliff. There was really no cause for alarm, the high water mark was some feet short of the cliff face, and the day was warm and pleasant.

And long . . .

After several rests, and several cooling, comforting dips, the ankle looked swollen and was more painful than ever, and the easily-climbed, not very high cliff might have been Everest.

It was a ridiculous situation to be in, but Elise was stuck until someone came and found her. Which couldn't be long, she reassured herself. At the worst, she might find herself spending the night here, since she had told no one where she was going, intending to be back well before Shard arrived home. But it wouldn't be very long before he realised something had gone wrong, and this was a logical place to search for her. Her car still sat at the top of the cliff and once that was seen it would be only minutes before she was rescued.

She dozed in the shade, but when the sun began to fade and a cool breeze sprang up, she moved into the last of the sun where the sand still held some warmth, and made herself a little hollow to curl into. If it was morning before she was found, she was going to get pretty cold.

Trying to forget the possibility, she wrapped her arms about herself and watched the gentle lapping of the sea, the tiny bubbles it left as it smoothed the sand in its wake. The effect was hypnotic, and she closed her eyes, the rustle of the leaves overhead and the occasional birdsong, the soft shushing of the waves combining to lull her into sleep.

She was dreaming, dreaming about the sea, and she seemed to be floating on it, just floating, but it carried her further and further from the shore where Shard stood calling her, shouting her name in increasing despair. She wanted to go back to him, but she was too tired to move, to swim, and she knew that if she tried she would never make it. She watched Shard calling her and she felt a soft, aching sadness for them both ...

'Elise——'

She opened her eyes and moved her head a little, and saw him at the top of the cliff, in his face a terrible agony of fear, and then he was plunging down to her so fast that she sat up, calling 'Shard, be careful! I'm all right—it's only a twisted ankle.'

He didn't slow down, he slithered the last few yards, hardly grabbing at handholds, and when he leaped on to the sand and strode towards her she saw that his hands were scratched and bleeding and he had torn his shirt.

'It's only my ankle,' she repeated, and he dropped beside her and touched it with shaking hands, then ran them trembling over the rest of her as though he couldn't believe that she was safe and whole. 'Are you sure,' he demanded hoarsely. 'You're sure that's all?'

'It isn't even broken,' she said. 'Only I couldn't climb back up. And there's nothing else—I'm fine otherwise.'

His hands touched her shoulders, and for a moment he closed his eyes. He cupped her head in his hands and looked down at her face, and as though the words were wrenched from him, said, 'Oh, God, I've never been so frightened in my life——'

This was Shard the impregnable, the self-sufficient—Shard who needed no one and asked for nothing. Elise looked at him on his knees beside her and felt a savage joy. Her eyelids drooped a little, and she smiled, a smile holding provocation and promise and a hint of slightly malicious triumph.

Shard took a breath, and said, 'Damn you!' Anger and laughter mingled in his eyes as he tipped her face to his and closed his lips almost brutally on hers.

She bore it well, her head tipped back over his arm,

her body passive against him. But when he raised his head, she shivered. His fingers moved down her arm and he said, 'You're cold. I'll have to leave you while I get help.'

'No,' she said. 'I can manage if you help me.'

'I'll hurt you——'

'Is that new?' she asked gently, and he winced.

'At least let me bandage it first,' he said. 'I'll get the first aid box from my car.'

With a firm bandage on the ankle and his arm hooked about her waist, half carrying her, Elise managed the ascent. It was slow, and when they reached the top she had to lie back on the grass while the wrenching pain subsided, but she made it. And when she made to rise and lean on Shard again, he picked her up bodily and placed her in his car.

'Do you want anything from your car?' he asked her.

'My bag, I suppose.'

He got it for her and locked the car, tossing the keys in her lap. 'I'll get someone to pick it up tomorrow,' he said.

They called at a doctor's surgery on the way home. He inspected the damage and recommended cold compresses, rest and a bandage. And then Shard took Elise home.

He helped her into bed and asked, 'Anything you want?'

'A drink,' she said, and he laughed, and went to get her one, returning with whisky for himself and a strong gin and lemon for her.

It wasn't until she began to feel lightheaded that she realised she hadn't eaten since breakfast.

Shard was sitting on the bed, sipping his whisky and looking at her. Elise leaned her head back against the pillow and said, 'I don't think I should have had this on an empty stomach.'

'I'll get something to eat in a minute,' he said. 'When did you go out there?'

'This morning.'

'Lord! You must be starving!'

He made to move, but she stopped him with a hand on his arm. 'Not really. Finish your drink.'

The slight movement had made her head swim a little, but as she sank back again on to the pillow, it cleared, and she felt that her brain was functioning more perfectly than it had for a long time.

'I should be sorry that I frightened you,' she said. 'But I'm not.' He looked up then, a lurking flame in his eyes, and she smiled at him. 'I didn't know until I saw your face then—that you love me.' Her eyes dropped as she went on, 'I know it isn't a word you like, for some reason. You distrust it, but I don't know another name for what was in your eyes when you found me today. And—perhaps you won't believe me, but no matter how it seemed, or what I said, or what you thought, Shard, I married you for one reason—because I love you. I was afraid to admit it, at first because the strength of it scared me, when I was very young, and I'd been taught to distrust my feelings and use my head. My feelings told me you were everything I would ever want, but I tried to use my head and I thought—I thought you might be using me. And when you took Granddad's money and went away, that seemed to confirm that what I'd done was the sensible thing. Only you'll never know how hard it was——'

'I only took the loan because I couldn't bear to stay in this country, knowing you were married to another man,' he told her. 'Your grandfather had offered me a stake before, but I turned it down. He used to give me hints and advice, when he discovered what I was after, eventually. But I did intend to make it on my own. It was his idea, you know, going into the Australian company—he heard about it through an old friend of his, and decided it was just for me. I owe him a lot more than money.' He paused. 'You made a crack once about not expecting him to get it back. I thought you were just having a go at me—you were in a malicious mood that night. Did you really think that I'd taken advantage of the old man and cheated him of his money?'

'After failing to get me to marry you—yes,' she said in a low voice. 'We all did.'

'Gary didn't,' he said quietly. 'I'm sure of it.'

She looked up. 'We don't see much of Gary these days. I suppose he would have put me straight, if I'd talked to him. Please try to understand, Shard. I had all the advantages that you looked on with such contempt, but I'd never been encouraged to have much faith in my own judgment. Even Peter made decisions for me, gave me advice. It seemed natural, because he was much older —and when we were married I was barely nineteen. I wanted to believe in you, but I was frightened. And then you never mentioned love. Do you remember telling me you didn't need it?'

'That isn't exactly what I said,' he told her slowly. 'I said I could live without you—I didn't say it would be easy. And I said I wouldn't *ask* for your love——'

'And that you had no use for love.'

'Until then. You're right about my distrusting the word. I knew I wanted you desperately, but I didn't want to give it that name. What we felt for each other was so real, so strong and deep—I didn't want to label it with the same word that's so often used to describe some of the most immoral and dishonest transactions between people.'

He saw the surprise in her face and laughed a little. 'I don't mean the buying and selling of sexual favours,' he explained, 'although God knows there are different kinds and degrees of that, and a marriage certificate is sometimes nothing more than another form of it. But the other things that are done in the name of love—women asking men to sell their integrity for money, in the name of love. Men asking women to give up work that they enjoy, that fulfils them as human beings. Parents expecting children to live their lives according to the parents' standards, and never allowing them to develop standards of their own even though they're grown. Children who expect to be parasites on their parents all their lives, lovers manipulating each other's guilt. People who think other people have a duty to make themselves miserable in order to bring happiness to those they're supposed to love. And people like you—who turn their backs on real happiness because someone says "I love you and you owe it to me to me back." No one has a *right* to be loved. It's something that's given freely or can't be given at all.'

'Yes,' Elise said softly, 'I think I'm beginning to understand.'

'I hope so. I hope you understand that I wouldn't beg you to love me, that I accepted the fact that you had other reasons for marrying me, and tried to give you everything I thought you wanted from it.'

'I wanted *you*——' she said. 'Only you, all of you. But you didn't give me that. You always withheld some part of yourself from me. The only thing you didn't give me was the one thing I really wanted.'

'I couldn't. Not while I thought you weren't wholly committed to me. Last night, I tried to make you admit that you were.'

'I am. I tried to tell you that before—but you wouldn't believe me.'

'At the time you didn't sound very convincing.'

'I suppose not. I was afraid to tell you the real reason why I was hesitant to marry you—that I didn't dare have faith in your honesty. You weren't being very receptive that night, and I thought that might make you more bitter with me than you were already.'

'In the mood that I was in then,' he admitted, 'perhaps it might have.'

'You've been under a strain, these last weeks,' she said quietly. 'Everything you've worked for is in danger, isn't it? I know the business is your life.'

'No. *You* are. If I'd been sure of you it wouldn't have mattered nearly so much. When I heard that I was likely to be involved in the crash, the only thing I could think of was that it might mean losing you. All the way home I was in a cold sweat thinking about you walking out on me because I wasn't what you wanted in a husband any more. And when I got here and found Cole kissing you it was as though it had already happened. Do you know how much you sounded like lovers when I walked in? Any other time I'd have listened to you both and known it wasn't true, but then the whole world was crashing round my ears, anyway. It just looked like part of the pattern.'

'I hoped you'd phone,' she told him, 'and tell me that you didn't mean it.'

'I had to put it out of my mind. I had to concentrate on what I had to do—what had to be done, I thought, to give me any chance of holding you.'

He stood up suddenly and walked a few paces from the bed, then turned and faced her, his eyes suddenly accusing. 'But you wouldn't have been here if I had phoned. You were with your parents, weren't you?'

'After the first morning—yes. I couldn't stand waiting for a call that never came.'

'You didn't tell me that you'd been with them. The first I knew of it was the next morning, when they came here and Howard offered me a job. And your mother said she'd talked you into coming back to me because it was a wife's duty to stick by her husband.'

Elise clenched her hand on the sheet. 'Did she say that?'

'Not straight out, but that was the gist of the hints she was handing out. I also gathered that she wouldn't find it entirely convenient to have a pregnant and separated daughter to explain away to her fancy friends.'

'I never left you,' she told him. 'I never had any such intention, and my mother knew it. I told her I wanted to stay until you came back, just a few days.'

'And she didn't lecture you about your duty and advise you to remember your marriage vows?'

Elise hesitated. 'Yes, she did, more or less.'

Shard's mouth tightened, and she added quickly, 'I can't help that, Shard! I didn't ask for her advice, but she gave it all the same, and it was quite off-beam and totally unnecessary. I didn't stay with you out of a sense of duty, or because of what people might say, or even because of the baby. I just couldn't think of being anywhere but with you as long as you're on this earth, and you want me.'

She looked at him steadily and watched the hard suspicion vanish from his eyes. 'I want you,' he said. 'As long as I'm on this earth, and beyond.'

'Please come here,' she said softly. 'You look so far away from me, and I can't bear that.'

He came to her swiftly, dropping on to the bed and taking her hand.

'Do you know,' he said, 'when I first came in today I

was afraid you'd left me. I wasn't sure how you felt about me after last night, and when I came in the place seemed so empty. And you left no note.'

'I expected to be back,' she explained.

'How was I to know———? I phoned your mother and a couple of other people, and Cole———'

She looked up, pulling her hand away. 'You didn't still think———'

'I wasn't thinking.' He took her hand again and held it tighter. 'I was too terrified to think. Then I went through your wardrobe and decided you surely would have taken *something* if you'd left. And in your workroom—you'd left those drawings scattered about. I've never seen them before.'

He looked up and she smiled. 'Do you like them?'

'I was too frantic by then to know if I like them or not. But I do know who they were.'

Elise said, 'I think he's going to look like that—our son.'

Shard's hands came up and he pulled her close. 'Supposing it's a daughter?'

'Will you mind?'

'I'll love it.'

She stirred and looked up at him, tipping her head back. 'Love?'

'Yes. As children should be loved, for themselves, not possessively or for what they give in return, or because they're an extension of their parents.'

'Yes,' she said. 'And if we haven't much money it won't matter. We can still give them the important things.'

'We can. But I forgot to tell you———' his hand was on her hair as it lay back against his shoulder, 'we won't be in receivership after all. I think we're going to be okay, with a bit of help from the bank and one or two clients who have faith in the company.'

'That's nice,' she murmured.

'Nice?'

'The way you're stroking my hair,' she explained.

Shard's narrowed eyes glinted down at her. 'Did you hear what I said?'

'Mm. That's nice, too. Does it mean we can have our house after all? And keep the land?'

'Yes. The house may be delayed a bit, but we'll have it. It's a top priority. An altered plan, though, with room for children.'

'I'm glad. I didn't want to lose the land. Although it doesn't matter so much, now.'

'Why?'

'I thought—it reminded me of our honeymoon, and I hoped that maybe it would bring us as close as we were then. Now we're even closer because we understand each other better than we did then. So it doesn't matter where we live or how much money we have. Oh, Shard'—her hand touched his cheek—'forgive me for the years I took from you, and gave to another man. Do you blame me very much for that?'

'Not now. At first it was hard to take. Later I realised that you were very young and I was too impatient. I scared you and you ran for cover. Too far and too fast, but it was what you thought you wanted, and you had the right to make the choice.' He paused and said, 'I'm glad you weren't unhappy with him.'

'I cheated him,' she said. 'He never knew, and I tried to make it up to him by being a good wife in every way that mattered. But in my heart there was always you. You were right—I had no right to wear his ring, feeling as I did about you.'

A little flame leapt in Shard's eyes. He kissed her with lingering deliberation, his fingers lightly touching her breast. Then he pulled away and said, 'I promised you something to eat. Aren't you hungry?'

She took his hand and put it over her beating heart. 'Yes,' she said, settling back against the pillow. Her smile teased. 'Aren't you?'

His hand moved warmly over her, his eyes glittering with desire. He leaned over her and murmured in her ear, 'I was talking about food!'

'I wasn't,' she whispered, and turned her laughing mouth to meet his kiss as he gathered her into his arms.

The Mills & Boon Rose is the Rose of Romance

Every month there are ten new titles to choose from — ten new
stories about people falling in love, people you want to read
about, people in exciting, far-away places. Choose Mills & Boon.
It's your way of relaxing.

August's titles are:

A WILDER SHORE by *Daphne Clair*
Elise had married Shard at last, and they should both have been
blissfully happy — so just what was going wrong with their
marriage?

MASTER OF ULURU by *Helen Bianchin*
On a working holiday in Australia, Jamie found herself encoun-
tering the forceful Logan more often than was good for her
peace of mind.

BETRAYAL IN BALI by *Sally Wentworth*
Gael's happiness seemed complete when Leo Kane married her
and took her off to Bali — but then he set about carrying out his
revenge on her . . .

THE SILKEN BOND by *Flora Kidd*
Lyn loved Joel Morgan, but what chance would their marriage
have when it would always be haunted by the ghost of Joel's
lovely dead wife Sabrina?

THE CHALLENGE by *Kerry Allyne*
Debra thought herself lucky when she was offered a job on a
cattle station — but that was before she met the exacting owner,
Saxon McAllister.

MAN OF POWER by *Mary Wibberley*
It was to keep him out of the clutches of a designing woman
that Morgan Haldane had asked Sara to pretend to be his
fiancée — at least, that was his story . . .

DESERT DREAM by *Rosemary Carter*
The only way Corey could get herself on to Fraser Mallory's
expedition was to disguise herself as a man — but she didn't
remain undetected for long!

LOVE BEYOND REASON by *Karen van der Zee*
What had gone wrong with Amy's happy and promising love
affair with Vic Hoyt? He had completely changed and was now
bitter and hostile towards her.

OBSESSION by *Charlotte Lamb*
Nicola had no intention of being just another scalp on womaniser
Lang Hyland's belt. But would she have the strength of mind
to stick to her guns?

THE SILVER FALCON by *Yvonne Whittal*
After six years' separation, Tricia had met Kyle Hammond again
— and knew that all those years had not killed her love for him.

Masquerade
Historical Romances

Intrigue
excitement
romance

MEETING AT SCUTARI
by Belinda Grey

Even Jessica Linton, bored with the triviality of Victorian society, was not prepared to flout convention by having an affair with a married man. So, to forget her love for Prince Paul Varinsky, she embarked for Scutari in the Crimea, as one of Florence Nightingale's staff, and found herself with the army that was fighting Paul's countrymen . . .

THE DEVIL'S ANGEL
by Ann Edgeworth

Why should Mistress Prue Angel seem so reluctant to encourage the handsome, rakish Duke of Carlington after chance throws them together? The Duke was certainly known throughout Georgian London as the Perfidious Devil, and renowned for his *amours*, but could an unknown like Prue afford to spurn his advances?

Look out for these titles in your local paperback shop from 8th August 1980

Doctor Nurse Romances

and August's
stories of romantic relationships behind the scenes
of modern medical life are:

PRIZE OF GOLD
by Hazel Fisher

It was the eminent surgeon, Sir Carlton Hunter, who
told Sandie that love was the prize of gold — but she
was determined to win the gold medal for the best
student nurse, rather than lose her heart!
Unfortunately, it was also Sir Carlton who was wreck-
ing her chances of winning either prize . . . .

DOCTOR ON BOARD
(The Path of the Moonfish)
by Betty Beaty

To meet Paul Vansini at the very beginning of her first
cruise as a hostess aboard the luxury liner *Pallas Athene*,
should have made Cristie Cummings perfectly happy.
And so it might have done, but for Doctor David
Lindsay's cutting remarks!

Mills & Boon Classics

The very best of Mills & Boon romances, brought back for those of you who missed reading them when they were first published.

In

August

we bring back the following four great romantic titles.

SILVER FRUIT UPON SILVER TREES
by Anne Mather

It would be easy, Eve told Sophie. All she had to do was to go to Trinidad and pretend to be the granddaughter of the wealthy Brandt St Vicente for four weeks and the money she needed would be hers. But when Sophie met the disturbing Edge St Vincente, who thought she was his niece, and fell in love with him, she realised that perhaps it wasn't going to be that simple after all . . .

THE REAL THING
by Lilian Peake

The job Cleone Aston had just been offered — editor of a fashion magazine — was going to be tremendously thrilling, and demanding, after her job as reporter on a local newspaper. But the biggest challenge was to come from her new boss — Ellis Firse.

BLACK NIALL
by Mary Wibberley

Everything was going wrong for Alison. Her job was in jeopardy; she was going to have to sell her beloved family home to a stranger — and Niall MacBain had come home. Niall, her arch-enemy, whom she had not seen for nine years but for whom she still felt nothing but hatred.

COUSIN MARK
by Elizabeth Ashton

Damaris loved her home, Ravenscrag, more than anything else in the world — and the only way she could keep it under the terms of her grandfather's will, was to marry his heir, her unknown cousin Mark. So she must be very careful not to fall in love elsewhere, Damaris told herself firmly when she met the attractive Christian Trevor.